Ed

Pulp Review

Vol. 2 No. 2 March 1993

Contents:

Copyright Information:

COVER: Painted by Sidney Riesenberg. Originally appeared on PIRATE STORIES 07/35.

Pulp Review - published by Adventure House - 914 Laredo Rd - Silver Spring, MD 20901

ISBN: - 1-59798-201-6
ISBN-13: - 978-1-59798-201-6

Review Topics

by John P. Gunnison

The second year of PULP REVIEW has begun and the number of subscribers is growing. I'm hoping that the stories being printed are what you want, it is difficult finding good stories that can be printed without paying outrageous reprint fees. This issue has a wide variety of stories from some rare pulps. JUNGLE STORIES, PIRATE STORIES and even a sports story from one of my favorite people, Michael Avallone. His first story that appeared in the pulps from BASEBALL STORIES.

"The Son of Long John Silver" is the lead story from PIRATE STORIES, published by Gernsback, this pulp didn't make it, as it tried to appeal to readers like ADVENTURE or ARGOSY yet at the price of 25¢. A much higher price to pay for a pulp in 1935. The author is someone who is unknown to this publisher, but the story I found to be pretty good anyway.

"Aw, Let the Kid Hit" was published in BASEBALL STORIES and was brought to my attention by it's author Michael Avallone. His very story in the pulps, it is something to behold, enjoy.

Lastly is a short story of only seven pages by Murray Leinster and published by Clayton. JUNGLE STORIES is one of the rarest publications by William Clayton. Being published only three issues, JUNGLE STORIES was canceled quickly as Clayton was having money problems and a couple of years later his entire line of pulps was canned. Although continued by Fiction House, JUNGLE STORIES was never quite the same as it was in the early 30's with Clayton. See you next issue in May. Get those ads in early.

The Son of Long John Silver

A Book-Length Pirate Novel

By W. R. VAN BUSKIRK

Fierce and Long is the Struggle of Lopez Silver, Son of the Famous Long John Silver, for the Treasure Buried on "The Dead Man's Chest"

CHAPTER I

GHOSTS OF FLINT AND SILVER

"WE are making good time, Darby." This from Conrad Dykes as we walked through an open valley in that disputed territory which was then claimed by both the English Province of New York and the French Province of Quebec.

I did not reply for my mind was taken up with grave matters at the moment. Dykes and I had been connected with the fur-trading company of Ormerod and

Corlaer for the last ten years. Dykes had been made manager in the woods and had made me one of his assistants. Business had increased; and although we had encountered each year the difficulties incident to trade in a wild country, murder had never been one of our problems until within the last few months. Some of our best trappers had suddenly disappeared and shortly afterward two had been killed. We had written the French authorities asking that they unite with us in running down the guilty parties, only to be told rather curtly that it was quite impossible to make the woods as safe as the streets of New York. Dykes and I had set out for Quebec to try to secure their cooperation.

The cause of the murders had us greatly puzzled. It appeared that some rival company intended to dispute the territory with us. But what company was it? And where was it located? The most careful search in this direction had yielded nothing but mystery.

For some reason my thoughts had been going back all day to the scenes I had witnessed aboard *The Walrus*, that ill-fated craft in which I had sailed as a cabin-boy under the notorious pirate, Captain Flint. I found myself frequently going over everything that had happened on that last night of John Flint's life, and at times I had fancied I could hear the wild cry with which he had summoned me, "Fetch aft the rum, Darby McGraw!" And now at the moment Dykes had spoken I had begun to shiver just as I had done under the glances of Flint and old Rip-Rap Murray. My state was partly due to the chill of the coming evening, but more to the fearful scenes which I had witnessed aboard Flint's ship.

It came over me then, quite suddenly, that the cause of our mission to Quebec might have some connection with the men I had known aboard *The Walrus*. There was, to be sure, no logical connection. My impression was rather a clairvoyant one—one that had grown from the roots of an older fear. I knew how foolish and irrational was my feeling. Flint and practically the whole of his bloody crew, including Long John Silver, the worst of the lot, had gone to their reward. And yet, I had been a sailor too long, had witnessed too many inexplicable mysteries, to put my fears aside as having no foundation. Some dead men I had known had had rather persistent ghosts. Alive or dead, any of Flint's men might be dangerous.

Time after time during the afternoon I had resolutely pushed these apprehensions from me. I had kept telling myself that they were but my old fears revived —the fears that had haunted me for some time after Peter Corlaer and Robert Ormerod had returned from their forced voyage under Flint and Murray. I had escaped with them at Savannah after the death of Flint and had hoped that I was done with the crew of *The Walrus* forever.

Then I had heard that the treasure left on Treasure Island had been carried off and that Long John Silver had taken his cut. I knew by this that the crew of *The Walrus* had hung together, and I could not help wondering what they would do about the nine-hundred-thousand pounds which Corlaer and Ormerod had helped Murray conceal on The Dead Man's Chest. Would Silver give up all thought of drying up Murray's cache? Not if it were humanly possible for him to secure it. You may imagine my great relief when gossip of the sea brought news that Long John had died at Havana in 1702. Long John would not come back in person to drag us off to The Dead Man's Chest to hunt for buried treasure.

But my relief was short-lived. Corlaer and Ormerod had made a map of the island known as The Dead Man's Chest and had indicated upon it the spot where the nine-hundred-thousand pounds had been concealed. Dykes and I had seen that map, and there was no knowing how many others had seen it. News travels, especially news of pirate treasure. And if that news had come to the ears of Long John Silver one could expect almost anything.

John was shrewd and inhumanly cruel. Even Flint, the most daring figure in pirate annals, had feared him. And when pushed into a corner, John had always bargained. At the last, when he knew that he could never hope to secure the treasure for himself, he would be likely to sell his knowledge for what he could get. A determined man in possession of that knowledge, and with means at his disposal to take advantage of it, would be sure to hunt us up sooner or later.

You can see what a state I was in and why I would be looking for danger where it probably did not exist.

I was gratified to have Dirk Monsma with us on our journey. He had no equal as a woodsman, nor could he be easily excelled in craft and strength when danger appeared. Just at the moment, however, he was absent. He had skirted a hill upon which an Indian village stood and had brought us to the head of this little valley.

"You keep to the path by the creek," he had said. "I will go back to smoke a pipe with my brothers in their tepees. I will find out what they know of this trouble, if anything. I will reach camp some time after dark."

"But suppose you are delayed and our fire has gone out," Dykes replied. "We are not much good without you, and you might miss us in the darkness."

"How many times must I tell you that I can smell a camp-fire two miles off?" sniffed Dirk. "I can find you no matter when I come. If I need to do it I can trail you by the sign you leave on the grass."

THEN he had turned back to the Indian village which huddled like a group of mushrooms under great trees upon the hill. I had watched his receding figure regretfully, for in my agitation it seemed that all our safety went with him.

Dirk was a man of enormous width and girth but as fleet as a deer—the equal of a dozen men in a fight. Now that he had gone, I began to look for enemies behind every tree and every turn in the path.

"Darby," said Dykes suddenly, "I don't

like this business. The farther we go, the more I am convinced that there is real deviltry behind these raids on our firm."

"Just what I have been thinking," I replied. "The Indians are not as ignorant as they pretend. They may have done it to get us up here so they can murder us."

"No danger from that quarter, Darby. We pay a little better than the market price for everything we buy. And we've dealt fairly. It is the best kind of protection as well as good business. We have a chance to select and grade right here in the field."

"But if the French are meddling?"

"Back in New York I thought that might be the case," answered Dykes. "Here—well, why should the French want our trade after we've boosted the price? They can get better furs at their own figure out of the north. There is more to it than that—something I can't understand."

The sun had dropped behind a hill and we were going forward under a crimsoning sky. I dreaded the night, for in my present anxious state I did not see how I could endure to travel in the dark.

"When are we going to make camp?" I asked.

Dykes chuckled, divining my reason for asking the question. "I thought you had been a daring pirate aboard Flint's ship?"

"I don't want to think of Flint," I parried.

He glanced at me quickly and I could see that his manner was serious. "Just as well not to. Makes one imagine all sorts of things. But John Flint is dead, I understand. His bones are in the river at Savannah and they will stay there."

He meant to reassure me, but he failed to do so. Flint was dead enough, and so was Murray. But what of Captain Billy Bones who had stolen the map of Treasure Island and fled with it? How about Black Dog, and Blind Pew, and Ben Gunn? I knew how unreliable rumor can be. Perhaps John Silver had not gone to Davy Jones, but was very much alive. Any of Flint's old crew on their own would be as bad as their master, and Silver would be worse because he was far more resourceful.

Just at that moment my fears caused me to see what I thought was a line of pirates running for the shelter of a thicket far ahead. I rubbed my eyes quickly only to discover that there was nothing there except waving grass. If Dykes had not already twitted me about showing the white feather I would have spoken of my impression at once. As it was, I held my peace, even though I had been quite sure for the moment that I had seen the red bandannas and the pigtails streaming. And though my second glance convinced me that I had imagined it all, I was glad when Dykes began to speak.

"You need not be afraid of Flint's men this far inland, Darby. They are sea-wolves, and they will stick to their element. Now in New York, or in any other place along the coast, there is no telling. I am told that John Silver has the courage for anything, that he can worm his way around all kinds of trouble with his ready tongue and his flattery. If he *is* alive, he may come back. But he would never need to come this far away from the sea."

He broke off with a snort. "How did we get started on this? Oh, it was you did it by mentioning Flint. Well, forget him. We'll find a Frenchman or an Indian behind this trouble."

"And he may be no less dangerous than Flint or Murray," I retorted.

"Certainly not! Not when we corner him. But he probably doesn't know we are here. Dirk took good care to keep us under cover. Even the Indians won't know until tomorrow. And tomorrow night we shall be in Quebec, if all goes well."

"Just the same I wish Dirk were here at this moment," I replied.

"No cause for worry, Darby. He is back there telling them some disarming story and winning their confidence. Not much chance for treachery when Dirk is on the job."

My mind grew more uneasy as he spoke, for his conversation had recalled a few items of sailor's gossip which I had picked up on my last trip down the river. There was a tale going the rounds that long John had been seen at various times after midnight along the waterfront. And certain men had been quoted as having heard the thump of his crutch upon the cobbles. Idle tales were these. But not at all impossible if Silver were still alive.

The sky had now turned to a deep rose and purple. The short scattered pines in the glades looked like men awaiting our approach. I drew near each one expecting it to leap upon me and experienced only growing dread as we pushed on safely.

CHAPTER II

Real Pirates

I DROPPED into a reflective mood about this time. I was wondering about Long John, recalling the meaning of many things he had said which had escaped me at the moment he had said them. I saw now how he had kept Flint uneasy, how Billy Bones had been but putty in his hands, until Billy finally saw through him and made good his escape. I realized with a start that John Silver had really been the brains of Flint's crew, perhaps the brains behind every daring and brilliant deed that Flint had ever wrought.

I roused from my meditation suddenly, for I had heard a sound like a human breath. I looked about me startled, seeing one of the short pines that seemed to move unnaturally. Then came a rush and I was crushed to the ground and felt great hands at my throat like a vise, strangling me almost into unconsciousness. What had happened? I saw a pirate's grinning face leering down at me!

"Make just one little grunt and I'll split your gizzard," I was told. After having lived with such men aboard Flint's ship I had no need to be told how to behave. I nodded my acquiescence.

"I'll just ease my knife onto your ribs to make sure," mocked the pirate. I felt the point prick my side. "Think you can take a breath without making any noise?"

My senses were dipping momentarily into darkness and the voice above me had receded to a great distance, but I managed to give a sign of assent. Instantly I felt a current of air rush in which almost seared my throat.

"Up with you," someone commanded, and I was dragged up to be pushed reeling along the path.

After a little I discovered Dykes being carried limp over the shoulders of two men.

"Are you sure you didn't hit him too hard?" questioned someone who walked alongside studying the still form of Dykes.

"Belaying pins are belaying pins anywhere and at any time," came a dry retort.

"Yes, but we had orders not to hurt any of them too much."

"I have hit men before," was the surly response. "I admit they don't need hitting a second time. But this one will take his breakfast regular tomorrow morning."

We were approaching a thicket of balsam some distance ahead of us. Dykes groaned feebly, indicating that he was regaining consciousness. My own head grew clearer with every step, and I was quite myself when we rounded the thicket to encounter a filthy, bloodthirsty group that waited there for us.

"Ah, Darby McGraw!" exclaimed a silky well-modulated voice. "Flint's luck aboard again, I believe."

I found myself looking up into the smiling face of a very large man. His oily manner and well-bred banter struck me at once as being a mere accompaniment of a very dangerous mind.

"Glad to see you, McGraw," the man continued. "You will take up your old duties where you left off. The rum is there beside that tree. Aft with it. When we are safe aboard we'll have plenty for all hands."

I hesitated, somewhat from bewilderment and partly from a strange fascination cast over me by this handsome soft-spoken giant who was evidently the leader of the pirate band.

"Prod him there, you swabs!" hissed the giant. Instantly I felt the prick of cutlass in the region of my waistband and a dozen sea-boots struck me and hurled me headlong toward the tree. I rose to my feet, felt about quickly for the rum, and was soon carrying out my old duties as efficiently as if they had not been interrupted by Flint's death and ten years of time.

I studied the faces as I served, but there was not one that I recognized. Who were these men? And how did they know me and the tasks I had performed aboard *The Walrus*? I could not understand, not even when I came a second time to make my rounds.

"I am glad to see that you know how

to anticipate one's wants, McGraw," purred the leader as I served him. "You will find me quite easy to work for, in the main. When the food is not to my taste I usually give the cook and my cabin-boy a bit of advice. But you'll learn very quickly how I want things. I won't need to explain to you very often."

There was a great guffaw from the pirates at this. But I did not need the laughter to let me know that I was listening to the hiss of a venomous serpent. This man was undoubtedly the most dangerous person alive. And when we were aboard some ill-smelling craft and well at sea, there would be plenty to make one's blood run cold.

The pirate leader rose and made his way to Dykes who had regained consciousness and was looking about him at the faces of the motley crew.

"You are Dykes, I believe," purred the giant, stooping over him. "I am Lopez Alonzo Silver, the son of John Silver late of *The Walrus* and, if the truth be told, of other ships before and afterward. I am sorry he is not here to greet you in person. He died two years ago, leaving to me his fortune and his unfinished enterprises. As a dutiful son I count it my first task to finish his work before taking up any plans of my own. As you may have surmised already, we are now about to sail for The Dead Man's Chest to secure the fortune left there by that gallant captain, Andrew Murray."

My heart sank as I listened, for much could happen before we raised The Dead Man's Chest, especially with the king's ships scouring the seas in search of just such men as Long John's son must be. And if we were successful in evading them and in bringing off the treasure, there was but little hope of our coming through alive. This man was undoubtedly far more crafty and cruel than his father had ever been. He would make no mistakes born of headlong action or of compassion. He was as cold-blooded as a snake.

There was only one source of help for us and that was Dirk. Remote as this was, I found myself depending upon him and listening for his approach.

"Ah," the pirate leader ejaculated as he touched me softly upon the shoulder to rouse me from my abstraction, "you are no doubt listening for the friend you left behind. I think you may give up the hope as of no consequence. We do not do things by halves. We knew you were on the way here long before you arrived. One can buy all the Indians he has need of with a bit of gold or a bottle of rum, and we got as many as we wanted. We had them watch you all the way from New York and report to us your progress from time to time. They are now waiting for your friend to approach. Meanwhile we shall send Mr. Dykes on ahead to wait for us at the river."

I suffered a distinct shock of surprise at having my thoughts read so accurately and must have revealed as much, for the eyes of Silver's son twinkled ingratiatingly.

There was nothing for me to say in answer. I stood dejected, numb with fear, and sick to the very marrow of my bones.

"Don't take it so hard, McGraw!" The smiling face had the appearance of kindliness and a great hand touched my arm. "This ought to be a welcome holiday after ten years here in the woods. There will be wind and tide, enchanted islands in the sun, ships and ports and white cities, and always the tang of the sea."

DARKNESS now descended upon us, thick, almost impenetrable. Dykes was quickly conducted down the path toward the river to the north and I was alone with the soft-spoken giant and his murderous cut-throats. I could see that the pirates held him in great respect. And knowing such men, I knew they had a reason for doing so—the only reason they would accept. They were ruled as such men are always ruled—by fear of a hand that shows no mercy.

At a word from their leader, they scattered and went creeping forward in the tall grass. Silver and I stood alone in the edge of the thicket and well in the dark. There was not a sound to be heard except the chirp of insects in the tree-branches and in the grass.

Thus we waited nearly an hour. Then before me on the ground I discovered a dark shape that rose suddenly as if out of the earth. An Indian had come with news for the pirate leader.

"The white man is now on the path. Be here by and by. I go back to help catch him."

"Good!" breathed my companion. "Fall on him when the time comes and truss him up. We must have him—alive."

The Indian disappeared as mysteriously as he had come, and Lopez Silver and I were alone once more. I waited tense, expecting to hear Dirk's grunts as his great smashing fists took up his defense. He would not be so easy to truss up. Men who tangled with Dirk usually suffered broken heads and a variety of other injuries.

Then I felt a tug at my buck-skins as if a bush pulled at them. I moved to allow the shrub or limb to straighten. I put my hand down to prevent the recoil from making any unnecessary noise. My fingers touched Dirk's great hands! Like the Indian, he had come through the ring of guards—had outwitted the foes who were trailing him.

He gave me such a start that I jumped back and jostled noisily against the pirate chief beside me. Then I broke into a series of low coughs to prevent my crying out.

Instantly a hand closed over my mouth and the voice of Lopez Silver was hissing in my ears. "Another sound from you and my dagger goes through your heart. I really have no need for you. And what I don't need I never allow to prove a burden."

"It's—it's the chill," I stammered. "The standing so long. Do we have any more of the rum?"

"Let me do the investigating," he replied. "You would fall overboard in this sea and be lost."

With that he went softly over to the tree and began to rummage in the heap of gear his men had piled there. Dirk reached out a great arm, lifted me, and began to move noiselessly. He skirted the edge of the thicket and slipped silently into a dry ditch some distance away. I marveled at his strength and speed and quietness.

Some two hundred yards to the north was another thicket and we were presently safe behind it. He set me upon my feet and announced calmly, "Now we get Dykes. Walk on the grass after me and you will make no sound."

"They will be after us soon," I whispered. "They will miss me and give the alarm."

"Not so long as they are waiting to catch me, Darby."

Then I almost laughed aloud as I pictured the chagrin of Lopez Silver who was now searching for me and did not dare make a sound lest he destroy his ambuscade. It would take them some time to learn how it had all happened. Meanwhile Dirk and I would be far on our way to liberate Dykes.

"But Dirk," I exclaimed in warning, "the Indians were trailing you. One of them reported to the pirate leader that you were approaching. He will soon pick up your trail and learn how you tricked him."

"I know," replied Dirk as we hurried along. "I heard him report."

"But you were not there then, were you?" I asked amazed.

"Certainly. I saw that snake on my trail. I watched him slip away and I followed. He led me to you."

"But do you really think we can get away from them?"

"You and I could get away," he returned. "But to get Dykes and get away—we shall see. We have already given them something that will delay them for more than an hour. Then they will need to go slow. The falling dew will make it hard for them to follow us."

We kept to the grass wherever possible, always taking care to obscure our trail. When we had gone far enough to be well out of hearing, we almost ran forward. After two hours of this, we were near enough to hear the conversation of those who were conducting Dykes. They were debating loudly and fiercely after the manner of greedy and impatient men.

"I say what is the use of waiting for Silver," one of them announced impatiently. "Don't we have one of the men who knows where the treasure is?"

"Yes, but we are not aboard ship," came the answer. "And even if we were, who is going to handle her? The captain knew what he was doing when he kept the bulk of the crew under his own eye."

"You don't catch Lopez Silver," said another voice. "Even if I were sure we could handle her, I'd be afraid he would shove up alongside some fine morning and make us all walk the plank."

"How is he going to show up once we get to sea? Where would he get a ship?"

"Where did he get the one he has now?"

"I don't know."

"No, you don't. But I do. When Lopez Silver wants a ship, he gets it. And he'll want ours as he never wanted one, if we try leaving him behind."

"But where will we be after he ships the treasure? Answer me that? How many of you are going to get your cuts and make port afterward? I'm for giving Silver the slip."

"If we can make them lose Dykes, I'd give a great deal to see the fun afterward," Dirk chuckled. "It would mean the end of the voyage for more than one of them."

"But how are we going to get him?" I asked, thinking of the dozen or more pirates all armed to the teeth.

"Follow them as you are while I find a way," answered Dirk.

He passed out of my sight, taking to the woods as silently as a shadow, making not the slightest sound that I could detect. I was alone upon the path, listening to the heated debate on ahead. Gradually the fear of Lopez Silver seemed to prevail, and the group moved along more amicably, having decided that it might be more safe in the end to permit the captain to manage the venture.

After an interminably long time, Dirk came back as silently as he had gone and apparently troubled. He walked beside me in deep thought.

"Have you any plan, Dirk?" I asked.

"No. It's much worse than I thought. The woods are full of Indians on both sides of the path, and they are following the pirates. I can't make it out, for they are part of the group that was sent to track me down."

"The Captain is keeping an eye on his precious cut-throats, I suspect," I answered.

"That's it!" exclaimed Dirk. "That's exactly what he is doing! Darby, I'll bet you were a good pirate. You know their ways. Wouldn't surprise me but you would have gone a long way in that line."

He chuckled to himself softly. "But it doesn't seem to help any," he volunteered. "We have two crowds to oppose now."

He fell silent for some moments. When he began to speak again, his whispers were drowned out by a rollicking song that went tumbling through the night.

"Fifteen men on The Dead Man's Chest,
  Yo-ho-ho, and a bottle o' rum!
Drink and the devil had done for the rest,
  Yo-ho-ho, and a bottle o' rum!"

The song had not ceased to echo through the hills when the sound of a remembered voice among the singers suggested a course of action to me. I lifted my voice in a wild scream exactly like that of the dying John Flint, "Ho, Darby! Darby McGraw! Fetch aft the rum, Darby McGraw!"

It was a long chance. Dirk turned on me furiously but paused as he heard the consternation among the pirates. The voice of Ben Gunn was wailing, "Oh my Gawd! It's Flint's voice! And him a-dying!"

In response to this cue, I lifted another cry and heard Ben Gunn and all the pirates go rushing madly ahead through the darkness. We ran to the spot they had just abandoned in their confusion, hoping to find that Dykes had been left behind, but he was nowhere in sight.

"The Indians!" said Dirk. "Now we shall be hard put to it to bring him off safely."

He plunged into the woods and was gone for half an hour. Then he came back to me like a great black bird floating out from among the trees. He pulled me into the forest.

"Here," he said. "They took Dykes this way. I followed and discovered the spot where they set him down for a moment."

We hurried on through the night, and although it was quite dark in the woods, Dirk's skill on the trail was so excellent that we made scarcely less progress than the Indians themselves. At day-break we stood looking down upon the St. Lawrence River, watching a canoe with Dykes and a dozen Indians turn the point of an island to disappear from sight. We had failed.

"Well, it will take us a little longer," said Dirk as he turned back into the forest.

We slipped into a rushing stream and waded for a long distance back into the forest. Then we climbed into the branches of some overhanging trees and made our way by this means into the deep woods. We breakfasted and lay down to rest. I was soon in undisturbed slumber and did not awake until it was almost dark. Dirk was standing beside me, smiling.

"Two boats filled with pirates landed on our island today," he remarked. "It seems that we have found their rendezvous without going to any great trouble to do so."

"How did you learn that?" I asked, springing up.

"I saw them, while you were asleep. Many things happened during that time. The Captain arrived in a terrible humor, but he purred like a tiger, especially when he learned that Dykes had been left behind. The men you heard talking so boldly last night fell on their faces and begged for their lives. They were almost dead with fear. That man! He can be terrible, Darby."

"So could his father," I answered. "No one more terrible."

"Wait until you see this man," replied Dirk. "He is a great big river of anger. His father couldn't be as bad as he is."

That was all until darkness came and Dirk led me down to the mouth of the little creek where he had built and launched a strong raft. As we stepped aboard and pushed off, I realized that he had not slept an hour. He had kept watch until the pirates had embarked for the island and had then made his preparations to try to rescue Dykes.

I did not need to ask any questions, for I knew our destination and what Dirk proposed to do. We were on our way to the pirate rendezvous; what awaited us there no one could possibly surmise.

CHAPTER III

"He'll Sink Us!"

WE touched the shore of the island in the shadow of some overhanging trees and drew our raft noiselessly against the naked stones where we tied up. We moved with the greatest caution, taking every possible means to conceal our presence from any lookout that might be stationed to watch for us. Dirk gave his instructions and was soon out of sight in the low scrub. I was to make sure that the raft did not drift away and was to fire my rifle in case I should be attacked.

I saw to it that the raft was securely fastened and took up my position in the shadow of the nearest clump of juniper. There I settled down for a long wait. An hour passed. Then another, and another. I began to wonder about Dirk. Had he been surprised by the Indians and captured? Not likely. Dirk had continued to live because he had been able to find his foes before they could find him. He was out there somewhere in the scrub trying to locate Dykes or waiting for the guards to fall asleep. The whisper of the waters lapping the shore came to my ears like the rhythm of a low song and I found myself about to fall asleep.

Suddenly, however, I was sitting up wide awake for I had heard something—a sound like a step as someone moved cautiously. I glanced about me quickly, being careful not to move a muscle. Was that a shadow on the gravel only a few paces from me? It was! And it was moving ever so slowly. I listened and could hear a faint sound like the sliding of a snake over loose earth. I decided that it must be Dirk who had left Dykes at a safe distance and had come on alone to make sure that everything was as it should be before declaring his presence.

"Dirk!" I called in a low tone. "Dirk, is that you?"

I turned my head as I spoke and saw an Indian crouched to leap upon me. I slipped away just in time. I saw him go tumbling and splashing into the water as he leaped at the spot where I had been. In my excitement I forgot Dirk's order to fire my rifle and began to club my assailant with it. I brought him down with one well-aimed blow and as he struggled up, I struck again. He fell into the water beyond the raft and drifted rapidly near the full sweep of the current. I sprang upon the raft and reached after him, but I was too late. The body sank out of sight in a swirl of waters. The sweep of the river had sucked it down.

I crept back to my position horrified by what had happened. The Indian had been armed with a knife and had tried desperately to stab me, and I had no choice but to save my life as best I could. Never before had any man lost his life in fighting me, and this fatal termination of the encounter left me awed and shaken.

I recovered sufficiently, however, to be thankful that I had not fired my rifle. Our struggle had been silent, no matter how desperate, and I was quite sure the pirates knew nothing of it. This would leave Dirk at liberty to complete whatever he was about. But what was keeping him? It was now some time after midnight and still he did not appear.

Not long after this, I heard a great shouting at some distance down the island. I seized my rifle, placed it in easy reach, and began to untie the raft. Dirk had been seen or Dykes had been missed. In either case I must be ready to push off at an instant's notice. I had barely completed these preparations when I heard men rushing through the scrub toward me, shouting and cursing. The voice of Lopez Silver vibrated clear as a bugle. I could hear every word of his hurried commands. Then there was a scream of pain and my heart stood still. Whose knife had sent that cry upon the night? Dirk's?

Three minutes later I heard a thrashing in the scrub near at hand and two men rushed out in full view. Dirk had succeeded; he had brought Dykes through without a scratch. They plunged toward me, pushed the raft out into the current, and clambered aboard, none too soon, for a half dozen Indians were upon the shore or swimming toward the raft.

"Row!" commanded Dirk. "I will manage the welcome!"

I heard his steering-pole making dull thudding sounds in our rear. A shape drew alongside, and Dykes gave it a resounding blow. There were groans and screams; a great shouting filled the island.

We soon drew out of rifle range and beyond the sight of anyone on shore. Dirk's small catlike eyes roved the waters. Behind the flat, expressionless mask of his face, his mind was working at full speed, planning how to evade any canoe that might come in pursuit.

"Keep them off the raft if they overhaul us," he counseled. "And stay on your feet. Don't strike too hard. It isn't necessary and it spoils the balance."

SHORTLY after this, we could hear the splash of swiftly moving paddles as the pirates combed the waters in search of us. Then, before we saw them, they had sighted us and were bearing down upon us.

"Ship ahoy!" mocked the voice of Lopez Silver as his canoe swept toward us in the darkness.

"Try to find out who we are," challenged Dirk, springing erect and ready to use his steering-pole once more in our defence.

"What port are you bound for, Captain Monsma?" asked Silver, his voice taking on a purring, patronizing sound.

"New York." Dirk's tone was as blunt and downright as the great pole with which he guarded our rear.

"Pardon the critical nature of my words, but your provisions appear to be somewhat meager for such a voyage."

"We shall eat when the time comes," Dirk answered, bracing himself to meet any sudden rush toward our craft.

"May I not suggest, since you are already at sea, that you join us?" inquired Silver with condescending politeness. "We have plenty of provisions, a good stout ship, and there will be no fighting. We shall get the bulk of the prize Murray took when he carried the *Santissima Trinidad*. We shall divide it, share and share alike. You and Mr. Dykes will get your part of it."

"You are kind," answered Dirk. "But if you don't mind, I think we'll keep on as we are."

"But I do mind," Silver declared. "Far be it from me to use rough means unless I must. We shall try reason and common sense, and we shall just drift along with you until we can come to some sort of amicable agreement."

"That suits me," Dirk answered. "In any case we shall be nearer New York when the bargaining is done."

"And me, too," Silver laughed. "The going is a little slow in that old barque you are sailing, but we'll get there no doubt."

Silver's adoption of waiting tactics had been dictated no doubt by Dirk's alertness and the great pole which he wielded like a walking-stick. There could be no rushing us until our attention was distracted; no birch canoe could hope to stand up against even one blow from Dirk's pole.

Silver lowered his voice and talked for some time with his men. They were either planning the attack, or hoping to leave the impression that they were doing so. But they were not fooling Dirk. They would find him as dangerous as a cannon no matter when they opened the conflict.

Two other boats now came up, and Silver called to them and fell back some distance, evidently to explain his plan of attack. Five minutes went by, and our enemies began to approach cautiously—

two boats on our left and one on our right, but all three still some distance in our rear.

"They will all come at once," Dirk declared. "And they will come fast."

I got my rifle ready. I would pick off Lopez Silver and leave the pirates without a leader. That ought to produce enough consternation to let us slip away. But I would wait for them to begin the battle.

Another boat came up and stood back at some distance in our rear. It was filled with Indians. Silver turned back when he saw them, and appeared to be giving them very careful orders. Then he resumed his place in the formation. The Indians veered off rapidly, pushed around us, and kept at a safe distance in front. They would come from all sides when the signal was given. In this way it seemed quite certain that we would be boarded.

The strain became intense as the moments passed and the attack was delayed. The pirates also felt the effect of the wait and began to move restlessly and to grumble in low tones.

"Sing, bullies!" shouted Silver, and lifted the song himself:

"Fifteen men on The Dead Man's Chest,
  Yo-ho-ho, and a bottle of rum!
Drink and the devil had done for the rest,
  Yo-ho-ho, and a bottle of rum!"

As the song proceeded, Dirk called back over his shoulder, "Look out when they finish it! It is the signal!"

And sure enough. "Now, all hands!" shouted Silver. "At them! Every man of you!"

The canoes darted forward like arrows. Dirk stooped down quickly and to my surprise picked up what seemed to be a great log of wood. He used it as a battering ram and struck the prow of one of the canoes a splintering crash, sending it lurching under water with all hands on board. There were swift cries of alarm from the men who found themselves in the water and Silver's voice was ringing high and clear, "Keep away! Sheer off, you swabs! He'll sink us!"

Silver's canoe darted away just in time to escape the blow aimed at it, but several paddles were lost in the excitement and had to be picked up. The third canoe which was filled with Indians, swept by our rear. After it had, we discovered that a tomahawk had cut through one of the bark ropes. Our craft threatened to dissolve into a pile of drifting logs, and would have done so had it not been for the quick action of Dirk who seized the loose ends and tied them quickly.

Profiting by this first brush with the enemy, Dirk now took up a position where he could defend the rear and both sides. The pirates were busy picking up their men from the shattered canoe and stowing them away. Half an hour therefore elapsed before they drew near enough to hail us again.

"You carry very effective ordnance on that old tub, Captain Monsma," called Silver, returning to his former bantering tone.

"It does the work," Dirk answered dryly. "And we have plenty more left."

"No doubt of that," Silver answered. "And you know how to handle it. You could send us all to Davy Jones if we came near enough, but we shall be careful not to do that."

"You learn quickly," observed Dirk. "You are a smart man for a pirate. You may last some time before you are caught and hung."

"Of course I shall," laughed Silver. "But you are not so stupid yourself, for a Dutchman. You'd make an excellent first mate on a wind-jammer."

"We'll see how we come out with this before looking for advancement," Dirk replied.

"You'll do well, no doubt. And—" Here Lopez lifted his voice like a trumpet. "And you'll do better!"

Too late we saw that the boat in front had answered his signal and had approached the fore end of the raft. The Indians were hacking away rapidly and would soon have us entirely beyond any hope of repair. Dirk sprang forward and sent their boat to the bottom, but Dykes in his eagerness to be of help stepped through a widening breach in our timbers and sank out of sight under the raft, carrying my rifle with him. I rushed back to seize him and drag him aboard once more, but he rose at some distance in our rear and well out of reach of the pole which I extended to him. In his momentary bewilderment he fell behind and was intercepted by Silver's canoe and dragged aboard. A great shout arose from the pirate crew.

CHAPTER IV

SILVER BATTLES A BRAVE MAN

DIRK and I worked frantically to draw in and secure the loose timbers of our raft which were being carried wide by the current. At last we stood safe and sound once more, thankful that Silver had been too busy picking up his Indians to interfere. We were now able to watch the pirates drag their allies in and stow them away.

"We cannot take them all aboard," said Lopez. "We shall let this last half dozen hang on to the side of the canoe and drift with us. We'll land them at that next island ahead and come back for them later. Shiver my sides, but this is luck!"

"How now, Captain?" he called to Dirk. "It seems you suffered a few losses and had to lighten ballast."

"Yes," admitted Dirk. "But things are not so bad. We'll soon be able to stop running and fight it out."

"Not now," laughed Lopez. "With Dykes safe aboard we could up sail and be off at any moment now."

"You would be back before a great while," said Dirk. "I am the only one of us who has seen a map showing where the treasure is."

"Then I am sure you understand that we must have you also," Silver answered.

"Yes. You need me if your voyage is to mean anything."

"And what I need," Silver answered in a cold hard voice, "I always get sooner or later."

"You can't make it much later," taunted Dirk. "When day-break comes we might run into other boats."

A roar of anger greeted Dirk's words, for the crew had evidently foreseen this very thing and were growing impatient and worried.

"Growl away!" snorted Dirk. "That is all you are good for. Sea dogs are you! You are nothing but meek little puppies. Now growl some more! I like it!"

Instantly there was a storm of profanity from Silver's men and their paddles dug deep into the water, sending the canoe forward swiftly. Above their angry voices could be heard the further taunts of Dirk as he fed their rage.

"Hold!" shouted Silver. "What do you mean, attacking without orders! Can't you see what he is doing? Do you want to drive right into his trap and have him shiver the canoe? I wonder that your mothers ever trusted you out of sight. In all my experience I have never seen such fools!"

"You ought to have a nice time together," sneered Dirk. "No matter what you do, it will end in the same way. It seems to me it was not a very good plan you hatched up, Captain Silver."

There was another growl at this, and Lopez saw that Dirk was turning the tables on him. Something must be done or the crew would get out of hand and the whole enterprise would come to grief. He commanded his men to fall back, and when this had been done, we could hear the angry discussion. Gradually, however, the voice of Lopez Silver prevailed. Then there were cheers and a splashing in the water as if the Indians were changing places alongside the canoe. Presently Silver drew near and darted ahead of us.

"Sorry we must leave you for a little, Captain Monsma," he called as he passed. "It is not pleasant in the water, and we have decided to land these red men on the island ahead of us. Then we shall be back."

"I understand," Dirk replied, laying down his heavy artillery and moving toward the front end of the raft.

Five minutes later I saw Dirk plunge the small end of his crude pole deep into the water. He cast an eye backward and sighed in evident satisfaction. Why had he done that? The matter became clear enough presently. His pole descended again, and there was a chattering of the Indians who hung to the side of Silver's canoe.

"Ah! Spearing them, is he?" Silver asked. "That is quite clever of him. About six of you ease off at once. He won't get all of you."

Then I saw what was happening. The Indians were diving and swimming back under us to cut the bark ropes that held our raft together. The other canoe was stationed behind to pick them up when we had passed over them.

I hastened aft to do what damage I could to the enemy. I was not a moment too soon, for I saw two Indians lift themselves out of the water and begin to crawl aboard. I struck them both and saw one of them go overboard instantly.

The other grasped my ankle as he fell and began to drag me off the raft.

"Dirk! Dirk!" I shouted. I saw him turn and spring toward me, but he was too late. Down I went, spluttering and shouting, into the cold depths of the river. My last glance saw Dirk turn furiously upon another boarding party which had taken advantage of our confusion. He had picked up his heavy artillery and was knocking the Indians off into space. A momentary glance later as I was seized by Silver, showed Dirk trying to tie a severed bark rope to prevent his raft from going to pieces.

HE stood up with a grunt of satisfaction. "Well, let me have some more Indians now, Mr. Silver," he announced.

"How about a little trade, Captain Monsma?" Lopez answered smoothly. "I admit that you got the better of us there. You lost Darby McGraw, but I can see that that is no great loss to you or to anyone else. Perhaps matters stand a little in your favor. What I mean is this: Let's call a truce and look over the situation. Perhaps we can make a trade."

"Well, I warn you," Dirk answered. "I've been trading all my life."

Lopez Silver laughed softly and musically. "And you've prospered at it too, from all accounts. I can't hope to cheat you, and I won't try. But perhaps we can make a deal for all that."

"Very well," Dirk replied. "Let's see what you have."

"It seems to me that matters now stand something like this," Silver began. "Here is Dykes who may or may not know where the treasure is. At a pinch we might make him remember all about it. He has a wife and children, I understand, and we have no desire to take him away from them unless we must. Now if you will surrender to us and go along quietly, I'll give my word to put him ashore in easy reach of New York. You'd get your share of the treasure along with the rest of the men, and I'd give you two thousand pounds of my share. Darby could go along with us as one of the crew, or he could go back home with Dykes. What do you say?"

I saw that he was indeed the son of Long John Silver and that there could be no advantage to us in listening to such blandishments. But I did not need to warn Dirk. He was looking the offer over very carefully. He hesitated just long enough to disarm Silver.

"What do you say, Monsma?"

"Well, it seems to me that you trade what you don't want for something you do want," Dirk answered.

"Certainly," agreed Silver. "Isn't that what we always do in a trade? Now you want Dykes, and I don't. But I do want you. I want you very much. If we trade we shall all get what we want. Then to The Dead Man's Chest and the treasure that we all want. What do you say to that?"

"I think I shall wait awhile," Dirk answered. "I may sink you yet."

How long the parley might have lasted I do not know, for at this moment the truce was broken. One of Silver's men had fastened a rope to the canoe and with the other end had lassoed Dirk.

"Pull, bullies!" he shouted. "I've got him! Lassoed him, I did!"

Dirk had acted instantly. He picked up his heavy pole and began pulling in the slack. The canoe was rapidly approaching in reach of his great bludgeon. Lopez Silver reached out with his cutlass and snipped the rope. Then without a word he cut off the head of the man who had so nearly brought about the destruction of the canoe.

"Pull, you thimblewits!" he stormed. He was instantly obeyed, for it had been quite clear to every pirate that destruction had almost reached them. No word was spoken now for some time. Silver was holding in his great wrath and his men were shivering with fear.

"I must beg your pardon, Monsma, for the interruption of the truce," Lopez began. "It was not a part of my plans. I suppose you will not believe that, and I can't blame you. We have a few bright boys aboard here who use everything but their heads. They would use them also, I suppose, if they had anything in them."

"Yes. I suppose so," Dirk answered dryly.

On the whole the incident was a fortunate one for Silver. His men now realized that they were pitted against a powerful, quick-witted antagonist. A single mistake would be fatal. They were now ready to go along with Silver and do his bidding.

"Watch him, back there," Lopez commanded. "He has a rope, and he'll find some use for it. I told you some time ago that he was as dangerous as a powder magazine, but you had to see for yourselves. You've missed Davy Jones twice by a hair. I hope you are through trying to fool him, for you have as much chance of doing that as you have of taking a king's ship with your bare hands."

His words sank in. All grumbling ceased, and the canoe was held at a safe distance. Thus we drifted along until Silver could think up some other plan to accomplish his purpose.

CHAPTER V

Monsma Gives In

WE kept on in this fashion until daylight. There was no further attempt to board the raft, and our slow progress became monotonous. But evidently Silver had hit upon another plan, for he had sent one of his two canoes on ahead and seemed to be waiting for it to fulfil his commands before he resumed his attempt to capture Dirk. I sat shivering in the cold gray light of dawn and was utterly miserable with fear and hunger.

I saw Silver studying my condition and looking closely at his men. There is a limit to endurance, and no group more quickly rebels against apparently unfruitful labor or discomfort than does the pirate crew. At bottom the pirate is always selfish and has no taste for something that must be won only after long hardship. I was quite sure that Silver knew this and would act accordingly.

"We'll be aboard our vessel soon, Captain Monsma," Silver called, after it seemed clear that none of us could endure longer without complaint. "I have sent for the long-boat and enough men to meet our need. I shall be very sorry if you force me to haul you aboard by the heels, but we can't dally here when some hostile boat is likely to come up at almost any minute."

"I understand," Dirk answered resignedly.

"It is not too late to trade," urged Silver. "Just say the word and I shall seal the contract. The offer is still open."

"I have heard of pirate's contracts before," Dirk answered. "And from what I have heard, I understand that every article is forgotten once there is booty in the hold."

"There is no living man who will say that I do not keep my pledged word," asserted Silver heatedly.

"I have no doubt of that," said Dirk. "They very probably won't live to prove that you are false."

"Well, you had your chance," Silver answered with deadly emphasis. "Now we shall haul you in!"

At a distance of about half a mile downstream an island loomed into view, and to the right of it I could see a boat making its way toward us. The pirates saw it also and began to cheer and to hurl imprecations at Dirk.

"We'll take you now, bully," they crowed. "This cruise will come to an end in short order! Better shoot all your big guns, my lad!"

As the boat drew nearer I discovered that some of the men carried long light spars which they trailed in the water behind them. What were these for? They had better keep them out of Dirk's hands, or he would make a mess of the long-boat in no time. As the reinforcements drew still nearer, I saw the men arrange themselves at intervals along the side of their boat. They were assuming what I knew must be a fighting position. Then the long-boat pushed by and the spars were lifted and made to fall upon the ropes of the raft. I now saw that axes were fastened to the ends of these spars and that the long-boat's crew was rapidly making a wreck of Dirk's craft. Already the timbers had begun to part and drift wide at one end. There was little Dirk could do except lift his pole and wait for the next assault.

The pirates shouted encouragement to the long-boat's crew and hurled jibes at Dirk. But my friend was not yet defeated. During the hours of comparative safety he had used his captured rope to advantage to tie a number of the central timbers together firmly. It would not be easy to sever these ropes for he stood over them, bludgeon in hand to protect them. Then I saw him strike. Only one axe found its mark but it caused a considerable portion of the raft to veer off and drift away.

"Will you trade now, Monsma?" inquired Silver in great good humor.

"I never trade with thieves and pirates," answered Dirk. "I fight them."

"At him there, you swabs!" Lopez shouted. "Can't you fight while I parley? Do you suppose I mean to let a man off who has held us up all night? Get at him and get this over!"

There was real spirit in the battle now. The long-boat was turned about quickly and brought alongside the raft. Once more Dirk almost saved himself whole, but not quite. Another axe had found a bark rope, and Dirk was left balancing himself upon a pile of heaving logs. As I watched him, I felt sure the fight was over, for it did not seem that he had enough under him to support his weight. But I was mistaken. He not only remained afloat but I saw him smiling.

"I guess your axe-men are through cutting now, Mr. Silver," he called out derisively. "Try cutting the rest of them."

WHEN I saw the last of his ropes protected by his huge bulk, I almost forgot that I was a prisoner. But I did not find it necessary to conceal my pleasure, for Silver himself burst into a roar of laughter.

"Doesn't seem an easy task at that, Monsma," he replied. Then quickly to the long-boat crew: "Take the other end of your spars. Push him off while one man does the chopping."

It required some time to organize this style of attack, and I saw Dirk shifting his weight and making his calculations. Then they were upon him. He put up a real battle and disarmed practically all his foes, but he was unbalanced for an instant and in that time the ropes were cut. In the fraction of a second before he went down, he swung his pole aloft and sent it hurtling against the side of the canoe in which we sat. The boat collapsed under us like shattered pottery and we went tumbling into the river. The long-boat drew alongside and picked up all hands.

"Don't harm him," called Lopez as he drew himself aboard. "We must take him alive. What a fighting man he is! With him at my back I wouldn't ask any odds of two shiploads of the rest of you."

He clambered over to one side of the boat as he spoke and took a look at Dirk who was floating by means of a log that he had managed to seize. "Might as well come aboard, Monsma," said Silver in a voice full of respect.

"Thank you, sir," Dirk answered quietly, "I'm coming."

"Don't any of you swabs lay hands on him," he commanded, turning to his men.

Dirk swam in easily and swung over the edge of the boat and sat down. He looked at his wet clothes and large blue hands ruefully.

"Well, I didn't win this time," he remarked with a shrug.

"Seems to me you did pretty well, even so," Silver returned as he cast an appraising smile at Dirk. "With a proper use of a number of logs you could have blasted us out of the water at any time. It wasn't in the nature of things for you to win against us, and the fact that you held out as long as you did was due to the bungling of some of my men. But come, Monsma. We don't expect to eat you. You are one of us now, and when we get the treasure aboard, you'll get your share of it. I'm like my father in at least one respect, I let bygones be bygones."

"Oh, I'll make the best of it," Dirk answered. "Nothing else to do just now."

"That's sensible," said Lopez. "We shall be aboard now in a quarter-glass and on our way. You haven't delayed us a great deal, and there's no great harm done either way. We'll need to keep our weather eye open all the way down to sea. But after we get outside, we'll spread every inch of canvas we have and go roaring along. The best way to avoid trouble is to get away from where the trouble is likely to be."

"How about stopping on the way to let Dykes and Darby land where they can make their way home?" asked Dirk.

"My dear fellow," Silver answered, "that offer was not accepted, I believe. But I'll still do anything in reason," he hurried to state as he saw Dirk frown. "There is a brace of king's ships cruising off Boston usually. If they sight us and give chase, we won't be able to land anywhere. The only thing we can do is to hope for the best."

"I understand," Dirk replied.

And he did. Silver had not the least intention of turning aside from his settled purpose of getting the treasure as quickly as possible.

CHAPTER VI

On to the Treasure

WE turned the point of the island into the south channel. I could see the pirate vessel moored waiting. It was a magnificent sight, a great tall ship as big as a frigate and pierced for thirty-six guns. Its long rakish lines and its high masts would give it unusual speed. It was just the vessel for the present business, for it could be handled and fought almost as well as a king's ship.

"Looks to be the twin sister of the *Royal James*," I exclaimed in admiration.

Silver smiled at what I said and nodded his agreement. "That is why I took a fancy to her," he replied. "*The Walrus* was a great ship, too. With John Flint to handle her, I'd stake her against almost any ship afloat. But for me—well, a vessel somewhat like the *Royal James* is more to my fancy. I like the eighteens on the main-deck, and I need the extra speed. I think you were present that day when Murray laid *The Walrus* by the heels off Treasure Island and was popping at her with his eighteens. If it had not been for the sudden appearance of that hurricane, *The Walrus* and her crew would have gone to the bottom that day. He had her cold with his longer range guns. My father never ceased to warn me on that score and to say that a hurricane doesn't come at the right moment once in a thousand years. So I selected a ship something like Murray's for safety."

"Where did you find her?" I asked, not realizing what I was saying.

"Ah! That is a real story, Darby. I'll not take time to tell it now. My father left me something—a rather tidy sum when you come to consider the sort of luck that dogged him first and last. But the story will come later. I suppose you have not encountered any of Flint's crew since you left them?"

"The last man I saw was your father," I answered. "He was rowing hard to overhaul Billy Bones, who had stolen the map of Treasure Island showing the location of Flint's cache. I didn't believe then that Bones could be overhauled."

"They didn't get Billy for many a long day," Lopez answered. "And when they did, he was dead. Of all of Flint's crew, my father was the only man to share in the doubloons when they were found."

"He must have made quite a haul," I speculated.

"Well," began Lopez with a sigh, "men are hard to satisfy, no matter how much they get. But he got more than one would expect. In fact, he did very well indeed."

"And he left you enough to buy this ship and start on even terms with the best of them," I supplied.

"There are ways of getting ships without buying them," Lopez answered with a mysterious smile. "And I think you will agree that this ship was worth getting, no matter how. There is not much danger of her being overhauled, barring accidents. Under ordinary sailing conditions she will go away from a fleet of king's ships without much trouble."

"And in a corner she ought to give a good account of herself," I replied.

"She doesn't require great odds of anything," he confessed, looking her over with pride. "Once the treasure is aboard her, it will be almost as secure as if it were in the Bank of England. And one does not need to worry a great deal about Execution Dock either."

We were coming up under her now and a hail greeted us, "Boat ahoy!"

"Captain Lopez Silver," called my companion. "Coming aboard with prisoners!"

"Aye, aye, Captain, sir!" came the response to be followed by a swelling cheer from all on board.

Ropes were run down to us and Silver went up swiftly to the deck. His grace and speed could not have been excelled by any sailor afloat, and there was about him a flair that fascinated me. What a hand he would make in a boarding party! He needed only the cutlass in his teeth to complete the picture. We followed him and tumbled wearily on deck.

I discovered that Lopez was talking to someone—a man with the most evil face I had ever seen, and I had seen the greater part of Flint's men at their worst—Blind Pew, Black Dog, Billy Bones, Israel Hands, and the whole filthy lot of the foc's'le hands. The sailor who was talking with Silver had a livid, ragged scar that ran from the outer corner of his left eye to the corner of his mouth. It was such a scar as would be made by a blow with a bottle or a flying splinter from the mast. It drew his face around into a hideous grin of perpetual irony. His hands were great heavy-boned structures which would be as effective in a brawl as a pair of belaying pins. His shoulders hunched forward like cliffs over the sea and his massive legs were set naturally for combat.

Some men advance from a sailor before the mast to captain by virtue of seamanship and resourcefulness. This man had received his advancement chiefly because he could beat a whole crew into submission with his bare hands. He had the kind of merit a murderous lot of buccaneers would be forced to respect. From the tail of his long blue coat a cutlass stuck out like a beam, and in his sash was a long wicked dirk. Silver beckoned to me and I advanced to look into the cold smouldering blue eyes of the man I have just described.

"This is Alan MacGregor, my mate, Darby McGraw."

"Ach! McGraw, is it?" asked the mate, with eyes that reflected the blue light of steel. "I have known no one by that name who was worth much, and I'm thinking you'll run true to warp even if you were on Flint's ship."

"By Saint Michael! Another Scotchman," I sighed. "The last time we were out we were dragged about by a Jacobite who dreamed of putting Charlie Stuart on the throne of England. Always prattling about Whitehall and his coach-and-four and a seat in Parliament. Then he died as pirates will, and left us to scamper home the best way we could. I had hoped that we would have better luck this time."

"Any mon who followed the cause of Charlie Stuart was unlucky," replied MacGregor. "I mind weel what I got out of it. But you'll no talk of him more, if you expect long life. His name is not for such Irishmen as you to be danglin' aboot."

He turned upon his heel and left me, and I could not help noticing that he behaved himself graciously toward Dykes and actually seemed to want to be chummy with Dirk.

"Ach, mon, ye are the braw laddie the noo," he exclaimed heartily to Dirk. "And if ye was juist to start rasslin' wi' me we would shake down a lot o' ship's furniture."

"No doubt," said Dirk smiling pleasantly. "We'd probably shove the cabin into the sea."

"Which we maun do," sighed MacGregor. "The Captain might be in it at the time. That wouldna be weel for the ship. But laddie, if only we had the room."

"I'll take him away before you make the mistake of trying it, MacGregor," said Lopez Silver with a mocking voice. "You wouldn't have a ghost of a chance, for he fought us all night with a club as big as you are."

BUT for a gleam of mischievous delight in Lopez's eyes this remark might have impressed me as the most innocent banter. But the gleam of pleasure was precisely not innocent. It went deeper. It meant that the captain was going back to something, something that existed between him and MacGregor. And MacGregor understood. Furthermore, he was by no means pleased with the knowledge.

"It's nae wunner ye look tashed after a night of it," MacGregor retorted. "I canna understand how ye survived it."

"And if you had been in command, MacGregor, you wouldn't," Lopez answered softly. "It was no place for a man who loses his head. You have plenty of brawn. And I'm not denying that you may be actually as strong as Monsma. But it takes wit and sense and self-control at all times to prove equal to this man."

MacGregor showed his good sense by snorting with contempt and turning to his duties. There was nothing to be gained in keeping on this tack and he was quick to see it. A retreat with some show of dignity was the best he could hope for and he seized the opportunity. But I noted that his covert glances revealed his smouldering wrath.

Silver led us off to our cabins and saw that we were made comfortable. Dykes and I were together, but Dirk was given a cabin to himself. It was quite clear that Lopez Silver did not mean that we should be so near the crew as to invite mutiny. Then he ordered breakfast.

"Welcome to *The Isabella*," he said, somewhat oratorically as food was set before us. "You'll find her a likely craft. She is as fleet as a grey-hound and as staunch as they make them. When it comes to king's ships she can show a clean pair of heels. As for weight of metal, she does not need to sheer off on that account. I have seen times aboard her when I would have given all I have, and all I ever expect to get, just to have Israel Hands at the lanyard for ten minutes. But we have a gunner now who can spot Israel a few and beat him. He can lay them down just where we like to see them go. And while our antagonist struggles with the mess on deck we can be doing what seems best to us without much worry.

"To be sure, we never hunt trouble. We stay away all we can. The fact is that about a year ago we had everybody looking for us high and low. It was no easy matter to find a quiet spot. Naturally we had our brushes with the enemy and our anxious times—days and nights and weeks of sailing with no port open to us. But gentlemen of fortune can find a way out, provided they have sufficient pluck. There are enough prizes to be had to keep the locker full, and when it gets too hot for us in one place, we can slip off and lay by until the storm blows over. That is just what we have been doing here. And while the king's ships were running themselves out, we have been getting ready for our greatest haul.

"Ordinarily," he continued, "one couldn't have held this pack of cutthroats in leash long enough to accomplish our purpose. They are a very impatient lot as you may discover. But when they saw that it was best to hide away somewhere, we had little trouble in putting the job through. It was not easy to stir up the water enough to draw Dykes out of New York and that cost a pretty penny in real money. But here you are safe aboard at last, and we'll soon be on our way. We'll lift the treasure, make port somewhere, and every man will be rich enough to stay ashore for the rest of his life."

There could be no doubt of Silver's enthusiasm nor of his skill in handling his men. I was convinced in my own mind that he had designedly brought about the condition which had forced him to go in hiding. It made it easy for him to keep his men in line, while he lured Dykes out of New York. A man capable of such guile would not be the man to fail in anything he undertook. His bid for the prize had been well planned and, if the emergency arose, he would be ready to spare no sacrifice and to fire the last shot in his locker.

A feeling of hopelessness took hold of me. We would not get back to New York for many a long day. We were seaward bound—on our way to whatever fortune Lopez Silver's necessities might dictate. He would not hesitate to cast us all into the scale—prisoners, crew, ship, and even himself. We would be fortunate indeed if we kept free of trouble and came through alive.

We heard a great stamping and pattering of feet on deck and slipped outside our cabins to see what it was all about. A whistle blew and there was a command from MacGregor loud enough to shake the hills, "Capstan men for'ard!"

Soon blocks were clacking and pulleys screaming. MacGregor was bawling orders to every quarter of the ship and men were noisily tramping on the forward deck and singing:

"Fifteen men on The Dead Man's Chest,
  Yo-ho-ho, and a bottle o' rum!
Drink and the devil had done for the rest,
  Yo-ho-ho, and a bottle o' rum!"

"Anchor a-cat, Captain Silver, sir!" called MacGregor a few moments later.

"Thanks, MacGregor," Silver answered. "Take her outside. We are on our way to the richest cache that gentlemen of fortune will ever find."

"Aye, aye, Captain, sir!" replied MacGregor, apparently another man from this moment and going about his duties like the sailor he was.

"We owe a lot to MacGregor," mused Lopez Silver beside me as we watched him at his tasks. "Without him to show us the way in and out we could not have used this plan to carry you and Dykes and Monsma away. But—well, I wonder if he ever knew Andrew Murray?"

He turned to me as he asked the question and his eyes seemed to bore through me. "Not to my knowledge," I replied.

He seemed to decide that I was speaking the truth, as indeed I was. "It could have been before your time, Darby. MacGregor knows how to keep his own counsel. But it will all come out by and by. We are off to the smallest and richest island in the world. We shall see what we shall see."

CHAPTER VII

Trouble Brews

We swept down the channel like a great white-winged bird. I looked about me, contrasting the order and cleanliness of the vessel with the usual litter and filth of *The Walrus*. Lopez Silver had taken another leaf out of Murray's book; and, more to the point, discipline was everywhere apparent. All hands from cabin-boy to first mate gave the heartiest, "Aye, aye, sir's" and hurried briskly to their tasks. It would not be easy to demoralize the crew, and yet I had reason to feel that things were not what they should be between the captain and his first officer. Down underneath, a fire was smouldering.

We emerged from the channel and breasted the full tide of the river with plenty of sailing room. MacGregor began to crowd her with canvas which took her down to sea with the banks racing behind us. I watched Silver, who was studying MacGregor's procedure, puzzled and suspicious. The very fact that the vessel was made to carry that weight of canvas proved that Alan MacGregor knew his ship and the river.

Lopez Silver's eyes, I learned, were the clue to his actual cast of thought. He might smile, let his features be tense or fall into repose, but the eyes showed what the mind was doing. Now as I watched his eyes covertly darting about the ship and coming to rest venomously upon MacGregor, I knew beyond any doubt that something was amiss between the two. And when I saw Dirk regarding Silver with unmistakable amusement gleaming in his small black eyes, I knew that my opinion had been confirmed.

"I think I shall go inside," said Dirk. "I may not sleep when we get outside in rough weather."

"Oh, by all means, Monsma," replied Silver, rousing himself. "Come and go as you please. Only don't try giving us the slip. We would not like that."

We turned into Dirk's cabin where we sat down with questioning glances at each other. "What do you make of that, Dirk?" I asked. He studied me slyly a moment and turned away.

"We are safe with MacGregor at the wheel," he replied. "It looks as if Silver doesn't like that. He doesn't care to be in some man's power, especially if that man is MacGregor. But he can't help it here on the river. And MacGregor displays his seamanship. It makes every man aboard see that Alan MacGregor could step into Silver's shoes and not cause a ripple in the ship's affairs."

Dykes came in softly and closed the door. He sat down beside Dirk and glanced from one to the other of us with level, searching eyes.

"Darby McGraw, you get some sleep while you can," he said seriously. "We may not any of us be in the mood for sleep by and by. Lopez Silver is stalking something down or I miss my guess. He doesn't intend to lose his ship or miss any other trick—not for us or MacGregor or any other living person aboard. He knows which way the wind is blowing. He didn't send me on ahead with one guard to watch the other that first night without knowing what he was about. He has been watching every man like a hawk since he came aboard, and he is back in his cabin now laying his plans to meet the break when it comes. I make the guess that Alan MacGregor will need something more than seamanship and courage when he lifts the lid."

Dirk had approached his bunk, but he turned back now, deeply interested, and sat down. He waited until Dykes had finished.

"You are right, Dykes," he affirmed. "The Indians have told Silver what his cut-throats were planning to do, and the men have told MacGregor how they feel. He is out there now showing everybody that there is some one aboard who can handle her. And Silver knows what he is doing."

"That is what I think, too," Dykes answered. "This Scotch grandchild of the devil may think he is smart and that Silver is a half-wit, or else he is ready to pull the trigger and let her boom. He had better watch however. He will probably get a whole broadside in his timbers before he puts Silver out of the reckoning."

"Oh, Silver will manage to rock along until the treasure is aboard," I asserted. "He needs MacGregor."

"I'm not so sure of that," Dykes replied. "As soon as we get free of this river, Silver can take her over. He needs MacGregor just long enough to reach deep water and no longer. MacGregor is a fool to show off like this."

"MacGregor is smart enough, Dykes," Dirk declared. "He tried to feel me out the moment I came aboard, and he was getting under Silver's skin with his talk of a little friendly wrassle. From what I could see, he learned just what he wanted to know. And now he is saying to the captain. 'You crack your whip, Lopez Silver. Any time you are ready for the music, I am.' But we'll not have the music until tonight or some time tomorrow. Meanwhile, I think I shall sleep."

We withdrew, Dykes and I, to our own cabin so that Dirk might be undisturbed. "Dirk doesn't seem to be greatly alarmed," I observed when we were alone.

Dykes did not reply for an instant. "Not alarmed, perhaps. But he sees what is coming, and he means to meet it, rested and with a clear head. I advise that we imitate his example, for when the break comes, it will be every man for himself. And there isn't a man aboard that would not cut us down without a qualm if his need required it. I don't think they will—as long as we are in the hands of the party that is likely to win. But if the group that gets us is sure to be defeated and knows it—well, we won't have a chance."

I was so frightened by what Dykes said that I could think of nothing to reply. After a short silence Dykes resumed.

"Let us see—MacGregor will be at the wheel today and tonight. By that time we'll be far enough out for someone else to lay the course. MacGregor will probably take his well-earned rest. After that we must be prepared for anything. Of course, he may attempt a surprise—may spring the trap when every man loyal to Silver thinks him asleep."

SUDDENLY so much talk about rest and sleep caused me to remember that I had not slept since the day before. I rose, yawned, and moved toward the door. I would take a turn on deck before retiring.

"Well, we shall see what comes," I observed as I unfastened the latch.

"No doubt of that," Dykes answered shaking his head seriously.

I heard Dirk snoring heavily as I passed his door. He would be ready for whatever the morrow held in store. I approached the rail and looked about. The river seemed as wide as a great bay and we were driving forward in midstream with the two banks almost as far off as the horizon. I saw MacGregor lounging at ease by the man at the wheel. At times he seemed to be in a doze. When he saw me, he studied me out of the corner of his eye.

"Better ye keep tight to the rail," he grumbled. "We winna stop to pick up any Irish lubbers."

I pretended not to hear him and strolled on. As I passed the captain's cabin, Lopez Silver himself opened it. "Ah, Darby, just the person I wanted to see. Come in a moment, if you are not too weary."

Inside I encountered all the elegance to be found in the cabin of the *Royal James*. I had not been told how Silver knew the *James* so well, nor under what circumstances, but evidently he had been deeply impressed by that dandified old buccaneer, Andrew Murray. I should not have been surprised if Silver had taken out a box of snuff and assured me that it was genuine rip-rap.

I spent little time, however, in looking at the furnishings of the cabin, for Silver's face was enough to hold any man's attention. He was white in spite of his swarthy skin. His lips twitched and his eyes roved about the room incessantly.

"Darby," he began, "you and I are all that is left of Flint's old crew. Yes, I was one of them for two years, then my father sent me to England to secure an education. I was to be a gentleman, ready to take my place somewhere in the Empire. It was after I left him that you shipped as the cabin-boy. I am told that it was you who stood by Flint to the last and cared for him when he was as mad as a March hare and calling for the rum every moment. It was that loyalty that caused me to ask you to come in just now. Ben Gunn is my cabin-boy at present, but as you know, he was Murray's boy, and I have never cared a great deal for him.

"I found him down on his luck and took him on. He has always wanted to be put outside with a cutlass so that he might be a regular pirate. He describes himself as being that sick of serving rum and vittles he is like to go off his head.' It suits me to give him his chance at last. You will go to your cabin and get what sleep you can. You will start as my cabin-boy tonight. I'll send word when you are to come."

He rose giving the sign of dismissal and I found myself outside in a daze. Was Lopez Silver afraid—he whose father had boasted "Some men are afraid of Murray and some of Flint, but Flint his own self is afraid of me."

I was too sleepy now to think long of Silver's problems. I made my way back to my cabin and threw myself down wearily upon my bunk. I began to recall the men aboard *The Walrus* and how I was called "Flint's luck." Then Billy Bones walked into the cabin and pointed his finger at me as he sneered, "Be off with you, you and your luck. Aye, it's fine luck ye brought to John Flint, wi' the rattles in his throat." I turned to get out and was confronted by the white face of Andrew Murray as he lay dead in the stockade on Treasure Island. Then we were well at sea, being chased by king's ships, and sailing—sailing—interminably on before the wind.

CHAPTER VIII

Silver Changes His Front

DIRK shook me awake and commanded me to rouse myself in a hurry. Lopez Silver had just sent for me to come to his cabin at once. It was quite dark, and a ship's lantern cast a flickering glow into the room. I looked about bewildered. Then it all came back to me—our capture, the ship, Alan MacGregor the mate, and the white face of Lopez Silver.

"Something is going to happen aboard this craft, Dirk," I replied sitting up and rubbing my eyes open. "The captain called me into his cabin this morning and made me his cabin-boy. Ben Gunn is to join the regular crew."

Dirk blinked at me, unable to conceal his surprise. Then a smile lifted the corners of his mouth.

"Yes," said he, "MacGregor has him worried. You stood by John Flint to the last. He needs a man like that, for he has many things to think about. You go, Darby. You may be able to help us, too."

There was no time to inquire as to Dirk's meaning. Lopez Silver had asked for me and I must not delay my going. I went toward his cabin certain that I was to witness terrible scenes before a great while, and, remembering Silver's agitation, I wondered how he would behave when the lightning struck.

I entered, and was greeted by someone who repeated over and over, "Pieces of eight! Pieces of eight! Pieces of eight!" I looked about me startled, and Lopez Silver laughed softly.

"My parrot, Darby. He belonged to my father who called him John Flint—after the captain, you see. Come on, you proud buccaneer and show Darby how you can talk."

A stream of filth and profanity flowed from the parrot's tongue in response to Silver's words. On and on it went as if it would never end. Then Silver picked up a cloth and cast it over the bird's cage, shutting off the light. The profanity ceased.

"They spoil him when I leave him on deck," Silver explained. "Every dirty swab that goes by gives him something more vile to repeat."

"Now, Darby," he began, giving me a serious glance, "I'm turning in for a good long sleep. Keep that door against all comers. That is what I wanted with you. Ben Gunn is a good servant, none better, but I wouldn't trust Ben if some one should go for him with a cutlass. I want a man who will last long enough for me to get awake and get my bearings. I think I need say no more. You know now that some person may try to get in here, and that I expect you to resist with your life. If any one appears, he is to be made to tell his business from the outside. Under no circumstances is that door to be opened unless I open it myself. If any one tries to force it, use this."

He pushed a pistol into my hand. "Keep that where you can get at it. Then use it!" Lopez Silver's face was so tense and serious that I could not help being agitated.

"You don't think any one will try it tonight, do you?" I stammered.

"I expect you to be ready for them whenever they try it," he replied. "They may come tonight or a fortnight from now, but whenever they come, you are to fire. And don't miss!"

He swung his hammock and climbed in. I paced softly back and forth over the deep rug upon his floor and wondered why he should select me, a prisoner, to act as his bodyguard. Surely he had come to sail pretty close to the wind if there was no man of the crew that he could trust. This sort of speculation did not make me any more composed, so I abandoned it for more pleasant matters. Silver began to snore, the surest evidence that he trusted me completely.

It was an uneventful night. Once I fancied I heard whispering just outside the door, and at another time someone passed, letting his cutlass strike against the wall. Silver stirred momentarily in his sleep but did not awaken. The hours dragged by and at last the ghostly gray light of dawn peeped through the porthole. The watch was changed outside and I could hear the men in the companionway calling out cheerfully or singing a snatch of song as they came on deck.

Lopez Silver was still sound asleep when the sun rose. As I moved quietly about his cabin, I was suddenly startled by the high-pitched cry, "Pieces of eight! Pieces of eight! Pieces of eight! You infernal dirty swabs, I'll break you all on the triangle!" And on and on flowed the angry words of John Flint, until Silver stepped from his hammock and spoke a few words to quiet the bird.

"Good morning, McGraw," he greeted me presently. "That makes a new man of me. As soon now as we can breakfast you may go to your cabin and turn in for the day. I am very sorry that I can't give you any relief during the night, and more sorry that I can't say how long you will need to go on in this fashion. We'll play it safe, however long it takes. and when we are through I shall see that you get a satisfying slice of the treasure."

I thanked him, since it seemed the only thing to do, and went to the galley for our breakfast. When I returned, I served Lopez and stood back to wait until he had finished.

"No ceremony between us McGraw, please," he protested. "It appears now that we may be forced to live together for some time. If you'll look in the closet there, you'll find that we are prepared to last out a considerable siege, if trouble comes. There are guns and pistols and swords in plenty. There's plenty of powder and balls, pikes and ropes, and belaying pins. And there are more where we can get at them when we need them. We are ready for them if they take it into their minds to turn against their captain."

He ate his breakfast hurriedly, and thus betrayed that he was in no little agitation. Outside everything was as quiet and peaceful as a summer morning, but I felt sure that he had not overstated the situation and that we might expect trouble at any time.

"I suppose I ought to look for anything, Darby," he went on. "Our acts come home to us sooner or later. And God doesn't need to have anything to do with it. Swabs are swabs anywhere you find them; and captains are captains. I've been a sailor before the mast and as dangerous a sea-wolf as ever graced a foc's'le. I know what swabs say and think. There is not one of them that would not help to pull the captain down and take over if he had the chance. I once thought that captains had the best of it with their marine law, or their freebooter's articles. I know better now. Captains live in a powder-magazine that is likely to explode at any minute. One misguided step and down they go with the whole pack upon them. With storms, and enemy ships, and shoals and plagues, and bad food, to say nothing of cowardly dogs that snap at their heels when their backs are turned, they have enough to try their mettle, and don't you doubt it."

I ate silently, puzzled and surprised by what he said.

"DON'T think I'm letting myself get out of hand," he continued after studying me a moment. "I've been on this ship three years and I've had the job of captain all that time. We've run down a gratifying number of prizes out of Porto Bello, and Chagres, and Vera Cruz, and Cartagena. And not a few times we've measured guns and sailing speed with king's ships and got through with something to spare. The captain's job on this craft is never easy at any time, but it helps when I can keep all hands looking for the next sail. It is this lay-up that has caused the trouble just now. It gives time for hatching up all sorts of dangerous schemes. I'll be glad when I see the last of this ditch, if we ever do."

"But we are at sea now," I replied, not understanding what he meant.

"The water is behind us, and the land."

Silver agreed. "But it will be some time before we get the slime off our scuppers. And mark me: We'll need to scrape her inside and out to make her step as quickly as she did before we went up the river. There is a lot of river-weed hanging on us and we may never get all of it off again."

He shoved back from the table and studied the cloth intently. His face had become ashy gray. He was not at all the man who had battled with me and Dykes and Monsma on the river—always sure of himself, always cool and mocking and jocular. Dykes and Dirk had alarmed me, but Silver's manner made my heart stand still. We *were* in for it! At any moment now we might expect the ship to be in an uproar.

"Whom can you count on?" I asked, breathless with apprehension.

"No captain of a pirate vessel knows that," said Silver with a shrug. "And it is only when his orders are defied or refused that he knows just who is against him. Usually it's too late then. It is pistol and cutlass, wounds and slaughter, and overside to the fishes after that. Even if the captain wins, which is quite unlikely, he must sail short-handed into the first port he can raise. There is no port anywhere that I am eager to make just at this moment, for the English and Spanish navies have not forgotten what we are like. It is that situation that troubles me. My mate seems to feel that it might be worth while to put me out of the way. And from his conduct since our coming aboard, I am sure he thinks he has me nailed down hard. But let him come! I have more in my locker than he would ever guess. So let him come!"

Half an hour later I went to my cabin and the company of Dirk and Dykes. I was now tense with excitement and in no condition to sleep immediately. Any unusual noise outside sent me trembling to the door to see what had happened.

"What is the word, Darby?" Dirk asked, after I had risen the second time in alarm.

"Just as serious as it can be," I answered.

"That is not so new to any one who has eyes," he retorted. "What about this son of Flint's old sea-cook? Is he going to sit down and wait for them to come and get him?"

"He is ready for them when they come," I replied. "Meanwhile you may be sure he will keep his eyes open."

"We shall all do that," snorted Dirk. "But he'd better see something to do. And he'd better do it first. It will be too late when they go to his cabin."

"I imagine he'll see anything that is likely to mend matters for him," I said. "He'll not miss much with his guile and experience."

We saw that we could do nothing to avert the disaster that was imminent. I think we all felt that it might be better for us if Silver's authority were not overturned, although we did not discuss this phase of the situation. We were much more concerned with the possibility of coming through the mutiny alive. We were unarmed, and could in no way protect ourselves. We were, therefore, forced to stand by and wait for the struggle to reach its conclusion.

It was not an enviable position to be in, and we did not take it with very good grace. Dykes sat staring at the floor, and Monsma paced back and forth, torn by many conflicting and desperate schemes. I sought my bed in the midst of their gloomy forebodings, fully aware that my position as Silver's guard practically eliminated all chance of my avoiding the fate that would overtake the captain. But my weariness was great and all my fears were dispelled presently in the depths of a profound sleep.

CHAPTER IX

Sail Ho!

I AWOKE an hour before it was time to resume my duties in Silver's cabin. I went on deck to exercise and to see for myself how matters were. I saw here and there little clusters of pirates in whispered conversation, who kept a sharp watch on the captain's quarters. As soon as they saw me, they began to move toward MacGregor. A fierce eager look was in their glances. Then they paused and turned about, some toward the braces, but the majority toward the foc's'le.

It had been the signal—this appearance I had made on deck. But I was early, too early for their purpose, and MacGregor had dismissed them. The affair had not gone to the liking of the crew, for all were sullen and some were openly grumbling.

MacGregor wheeled to face the outspoken ones, his eyes glowing like two flaming torches.

"Ye'll stow that, ye clapper-tongued devils!" he stormed at them. "Another sound out of ye and ye'll be carrying your gizzards in your hands!"

There was no further sound from the men and I was relieved to know that the fatal moment had been postponed. But the incident sufficed to show me how desperate was our situation. The crew would be with MacGregor to a man when the time came.

Meanwhile Silver kept to his cabin or ventured out only when he was quite sure of getting back safely. This was a mistake, I felt. This was a time for boldness. The proper amount of daring, a firm bearding of this pack of wolves on deck, would go far toward meeting the dominance of the mate. And if Silver were to call MacGregor out and fight him, he could very probably win back his ship and his crew.

I was just turning toward my quarters when there came a hail from the man in the fore-top.

"Sail ho! South by east!"

Men came tumbling up the companionway and from all parts of the deck to get a look. MacGregor quickly leveled his glasses in the direction indicated. I went forward in the wake of the rush and stood by the rail peering off into endless wastes of water. I could see no sign of a vessel anywhere.

"Schooner ahead!" called the lookout. Then I saw her, a three-masted schooner, with sails like flame in the afternoon sunlight, hurrying toward us like a great golden bird skimming the waves. I held my breath as I watched her, for she seemed too beautiful to be something made by man. Her captain evidently believed that *The Isabella* was a king's ship, for he seemed to veer more in our direction.

"A merchantman," I heard MacGregor announce. "Too bad that we must let her go."

The distance between the two vessels shortened rapidly and it was not long until the crew had made out the nature of the craft drawing nearer. A great cheer went up which showed me that every man expected the order to attack. Men ran for their cutlasses and the gun-crews tumbled over one another in getting to their places. Boarding parties sprang forward dancing like hungry wolves and shouting their lust for plunder.

MacGregor's voice rang high and clear above the tumult. "Ye'll no be attacking! Back to your places! Dinna ye hear me say we tak but one prize this trip?"

A low ominous growl greeted his words, and the mate drew his cutlass. He turned upon them with murder in his eye.

"One more word will be the last for some of ye," he announced.

His voice could be heard everywhere in the ship. A hush came over the men as they hung between open revolt and knuckling under.

At that precise moment I saw Lopez Silver come out of his cabin and walk slowly and with great dignity toward MacGregor and the snarling crew. He looked casually out to sea at the approaching vessel, let his glance run over the deck, taking in the exact situation, then, as if nothing had ever been amiss, he assumed command.

"Gun-crews to your places!" he ordered in a calm voice. "Powder monkeys ready for orders! Stand by to go into action!"

HIS words were as a lighted match applied to powder. The mutinous crew which had up to this moment been ready to fly at his throat at a word from MacGregor cheered him to a man. There was rushing and tumbling into places. There were screams of delight and wild cries. Then a great half-naked man swung his cutlass high above his head and led three cheers for Captain Lopez Silver. It had been done without striking a blow.

"Fire when you are ready, Cowden," Silver called to his chief gunner.

MacGregor's face was a study. Rage, chagrin, hate, alarm, and terrible fear showed for every man to see. He kept his distance from Silver expecting, as well he might, that the captain would hew him in pieces. His chance had disappeared in an instant, had dissolved in one fatal miscalculation.

"Captain," he almost shouted. "Captain Silver, sir! I misunderstood you, sir! I thought you winna tak a prize until after we'd shipped the treasure!"

"To your place, MacGregor," Silver replied ignoring the mate's excited manner.

His tone was that of a man who is master of his ship and has every man ready to do his bidding. "You forget yourself, sir. You are to have the honor of leading the boarding party as usual!"

MacGregor hurried off. His face was a grayish purple, but his eyes revealed his eagerness to escape an awkward situation at any price. He had lost, but he was still alive. The eighteens roared and the whole deck was a shouting tumult of unrestricted exultation.

"A hit! A hit! And only the first shot!" screamed the milling crew. Silver looked upon them with a benevolent smile. The merchantman now sheered off. The eighteens roared again. The foremast came tumbling down upon the deck of the ill-fated vessel and went looping overside. One could hear nothing on Silver's deck after that, for the pirates went mad with joy. Then the broadside from our vessel tossed us about on a quivering deck.

We were drawing in close now and the eighteens were pounding like a hammer and its echo. The merchantman was helpless but making a fight of it. A ball groaned across our deck and carried three men with it, scattering portions of their dismembered bodies to mark its wake. Another sank with splintering force in the hull a few feet above the water-line. A second broadside was Silver's response. The eighteens brought down another mast and made the deck a pile of yards and sails.

During all this time Silver did not permit his eyes to wander from MacGregor. With his hand on a loaded pistol he waited until we had come near the helpless merchantman. Then he ordered the grappling irons to be made ready and a boarding party formed. There was something ominous and determined in his manner, something of the cat ready to spring upon a victim.

Then when the irons went home and the sea-wolves under the command of MacGregor went over with cheers and terrifying shouts, I saw Lopez draw his weapon. His eyes were like pin-points and his face was twisted into a cruel sneer. There was now a rattle of small arms, the screams of wounded men, and the silver licking of the cutlasses on the deck of the merchantman. Silver's pistol cracked suddenly at my side and simultaneously I saw MacGregor go down in a heap.

The men aboard our craft had all crowded to the rail for the next wave of the attack. When they saw MacGregor fall, they plunged forward without orders and quickly put an end to all resistance. Silver quietly reloaded his pistol and strode forward to take formal possession of the prize. There was no one to meet him except the members of his own crew, for the pirates in their rage at what had happened to MacGregor had not left one man alive upon the captured ship.

She was a rich haul, for she carried a considerable amount of money as well as foodstuffs and delicacies of every kind. The pirates carried the wounded MacGregor aboard *The Isabella* and turned him over to the surgeon. He was dangerously wounded, and just at first the surgeon was not inclined to be encouraging. After examining the wound more carefully, and dressing it, he expressed the opinion that MacGregor might have a chance.

The plunderers now began stripping the captured vessel of its stores. Clothing, arms, money, food, rum, and even the uninjured sails and yards were stored away on *The Isabella.* The labor consumed practically the whole of the night, and dawn was streaking the eastern sky when the powder train was laid and we drew off. There was a little later a rending, booming crash somewhere behind us in the shadows. When daylight came there was not even a floating spar to mark the spot where the vessel had gone down.

CHAPTER X

Silver Takes Command

SILVER now called his men to the mast and made an allotment of the booty according to the articles of agreement. He made a speech commending the men for their patience during the last year and their courage now in the thick of battle. He expressed just the right amount of regret that MacGregor had been wounded and dwelt just long enough on the mate's virtues. He was given a hearty cheer when he concluded, and another and more hearty one when he ordered up a keg of rum for all hands. They were to help themselves. No restrictions would be enforced so long as the vessel was kept under way. He left them in great glee, shouting the praises of their captain and roaring out the rollicking songs of the sea.

Silver gave me an almost happy smile as he motioned me toward his cabin. When we were inside he cast aside his cutlass and sprawled at ease in a comfortable chair.

"Well," he said, "I am the master again. Too bad about MacGregor. He is a good mate and deserved better than he got."

He winked at me and made a wry face. "Bunglers!" he ejaculated. "The crews of merchantmen never can handle a pistol. As close as they were they should have drilled him through. Oh, well, it will be some time before he swaggers on deck to take over the watch. And in the meantime we'll ship the treasure and divide it according to terms."

He was in great fettle now and I marveled at the change in him. Only twenty-four hours ago he had been as desperate as a pirate leader ever gets. No doubt he had remained in that condition until the moment when he had heard MacGregor call off the attack. Fate had been kind to Lopez Silver and he had risen to the opportunity in every way—except in his bad shot at MacGregor.

My services were now no longer required, for both Silver and I could come and go as we pleased. I lost little time in getting to my cabin, where I found both Dykes and Dirk bursting with questions.

"What happened?" asked Dirk. "Mr. Silver had us sent below and we saw nothing."

I told them as best I could what had happened, not forgetting to mention Silver's dramatic appearance at the right moment, MacGregor's fear and rage, and Silver's one shot at the defenders of the schooner. When I had finished my recital, my two friends sat in silent wonder.

"I told you MacGregor would need more than courage to get the better of the Captain," burst out Dykes. "Clever of Silver, that. Now he is on his way with the crew behind him to a man after this rich haul. If he keeps them aboard with money in their pockets, they'll follow him to any length. And, with just the right amount of rum, they will be hard for any ship of the line to crack."

"MacGregor is a fool," Dirk put in. "Over a year laid up. These devils thirsty for blood and gold, and MacGregor orders them not to fight. Makes me wonder if it was not someone else who shot him. Silver could have missed him altogether at that distance."

"I'm quite sure Silver tried to hit him," I answered. "I saw his face before it happened. He was just waiting his chance."

"And someone else may have been waiting, too," Dirk answered. "Just the same I hope MacGregor gets well. We may need him later on."

Silver laid his course a little west of south, cutting across the course of all west-bound ships. The crew was cocky, every man singing at his turn and quick to respond heartily, "Aye aye, Captain Silver, sir!" And what amazed me was the unmistakable affection in which they seemed to regard him.

But I gradually came to understand. He had promised them safety, money in their pockets, good treatment, and an easy lay. He had kept his word. And being at heart children, in spite of their cruelties, they honored him. It would take a great deal of blundering now to wean them away from Silver, and he had showed himself to be a man who seldom blundered.

It soon became known to all on board that MacGregor was not doing as well as he should. He continued delirious, and the surgeon was doubtful of his final recovery unless we remained in the northern latitudes for at least another month. To take him at once to the heat of the tropics would certainly prove fatal. Silver appeared now to grow grave and thoughtful as if hesitating as to what course he should take, but I noticed that a full press of canvas carried us farther south every day.

The buccaneers shook their heads gravely whenever MacGregor's name was mentioned, but no one made the suggestion that we should remain north to save the mate's life. They were gentlemen of fortune—the human wolf-pack on the hunt. If some of their number should be pulled down—well, it was the price one must pay.

When any one mentioned MacGregor to Silver he would appear to grow much distressed. He would walk rapidly away and turn back in nervous fashion saying, "We ought to save him if we can. It's inhuman to go on. But what can we do? A lot of people have heard of Murray's cache on The Dead Man. Almost all of you had heard of it before coming to me. If someone goes to look for it they might stumble upon it. We might wait here just long enough for them to ship it and get away."

I saw through Silver's words to his own secret desire, but I was sure that what he had said would not fail to have its effect upon his greedy crew. It was not to be expected that they would permit any man to keep them from securing the treasure, now that there was a reasonable chance of bringing it aboard.

ON the second day after this conversation we raised the Bermudas an hour after nightfall. MacGregor was better, very much better, but it was still quite clear that he would be unable to endure the rigors of the tropics immediately. And haste seemed to every man aboard to be absolutely essential to our success. Silver called all hands to the mast to decide what ought to be done.

The conference was long and very solemn. Silver made again just the kind of speech that would conceal his own heartlessness, while leaving the crew no choice but to go on. At last they left the decision to him. He was their leader. Whatever he thought best would suit all hands.

Lopez Silver stood in profound silence for a full minute as if it were no easy matter to reach a satisfactory conclusion.

"We could put him ashore," he began hesitatingly. "With his share of the prize-money we have just secured he would be quite comfortable until he could ship aboard some honest vessel. To take him with us—well, that wouldn't be fair—wouldn't be in keeping with what I promised him when I took him on. I think we'll send him ashore tonight and leave him in good hands."

The idea met with the approval of the entire crew, and all present seemed much relieved to find such an easy way out of the difficulty. We stood in nearer shore about ten o'clock that night. A boat went overside. MacGregor was brought up from the sick-bay and placed in a litter which would swing him over and down into the waiting boat.

"It's this or certain death for you, MacGregor," said Silver standing over him in a grave reflective mood. "We regard you as a fine officer and shipmate, too fine to be sacrificed unnecessarily when there is a chance of saving your life. We regret exceedingly that you won't be with us to share in the treasure, but you would not last long enough for that if we took you along. We felt you would rather be alive than to be dropped overside to Davy Jones. Good-bye, and the best of luck."

MacGregor said little. His perplexity was evident, for he could not know that they were not taking him ashore to murder him. One thing was absolutely clear to him. Silver was using this ruse to get him out of the way.

"It's all right, Captain Silver, sir," he replied weakly. "You know weel I'm in no shape to be choosin' or refusin'. But if I live, we'll meet again. And we maun talk over the days agone, ye ken that weel."

"It will be a pleasure to look forward to, MacGregor," Silver replied in a kindly tone but with eyes that glinted mockingly at the helpless man before him. "And may it be at no distant date."

MacGregor was too weak to engage Silver long in this sort of battle. He turned his eyes dumbly away and signaled that he was ready to depart.

The boat returned shortly afterward. MacGregor had been turned over to kindly people who lived in a clean little cottage fronting the shore. There in this mild climate he would mend quickly. Everyone was rejoiced and perhaps a little envious that he was out of the ship and free of the perils of a gentleman of fortune. The ship was put under way on a southerly course.

Silver took me to his cabin where he ordered a noggin of rum and drank to the success of our venture.

"It's been a long shot, first and last," he mused aloud. "I saw that I had made a mistake on MacGregor almost at once. I knew of course that he would want all he could get, but I didn't regard him as a man who would come so near to taking everything. A little more 'cossetting to the men,' as he called it, and he could have sent me overside in an open boat or dropped me in the sea. The only mistake he ever made, to my knowledge, was in refusing to give the men their chance at this last prize.

"It was good sense in a way, too, but it was fatal for all that. It takes more than just good sense to get along as leader of this pack. One needs a sense of the moods and wishes and fears of the men under him. And it's always good business to slack the rein when it can do no lasting harm. That is where MacGregor failed."

He leaned forward with his elbows upon the table and lapsed into deep thought. Outside the night was as clear as daylight and a good wind whistled in the shrouds. We were on our way to bring Murray's treasure aboard and were destined to have many adventures in doing it.

CHAPTER XI

Silver Talks

SILVER now laid our course south-south-east. This he did in order to get "the trades" far beyond the danger zone. Then he could turn westward and run before the wind just south of the beaten track of all vessels plying between Europe and the West Indies.

This tack consumed a great deal of time and made the pirates restive, although every man could see the wisdom of Silver's action. It was dangerous dodging about among the islands off Cuba and Hispaniola, especially when there was no way of knowing the actual status of friendship between the several nations. After being out of the way of news for a year, it was far wiser to run the least possible risk. We, therefore, sailed far to the east of the islands of the Caribbean until we had reached a latitude that would let us come back with the wind to The Dead Man.

The passage was uneventful for the most part. The sky was clear and the wind bracing day after day. With supplies at the peak and all lockers full, we were a healthy and well fed lot. Except for one or two suspicious signs we might have been taken for a king's ship, so clean was the vessel and so smart was the discipline at all hours.

One had but to cross Silver's deck to know immediately that he was a captain of the great tradition and could sail his ship against the best men afloat. I found myself wondering just how he had come by this knowledge, for I had reason to know that his father had not been over certain of being able to lay a course. Out it came one day—the answer to this and many other questions. We had just made our most easterly point and had turned to go racing westward.

"We are on the last leg of the outbound passage," said Silver as he scanned the map upon the table in his cabin. "We are just here at this moment, and we shall go on our present course to this spot which happens to be The Dead Man's Chest. I have paid plenty to learn the trick of navigating with that degree of certainty. My father left me a light schooner among other things of value and I sailed it for some time in legitimate business. It was the only way to learn and be sure of avoiding suspicion while I was learning. I was soon able to handle a ship, to judge men, and to make plans that would not turn out disastrously.

"When I had made this amount of progress I began to assemble a crew of just the kind that suited my ultimate purpose. You may be sure I had no little trouble holding such men in hand. It was hard to keep them from taking over, and harder to keep from wanting to move too fast myself. But I went slow and learned the knack of reading the state of my men at any moment. After I had gone far enough to ride out a few tornadoes, find myself, and get home safely, I knew that I could turn loose any time I cared to do so."

He sat down now, sipped at a noggin of rum, growing more confidential all the while. He was at last in striking distance of his goal and had already begun to think of himself as successful. He looked back from his achievement and wanted me to share his pleasure. I found it easy to pardon him. He had come no little distance and was no doubt entitled to the satisfaction his ability yielded.

"One day we slipped our cables and went for a prize," he resumed. "We continued to play it safe, for my ship was too small to run any great risk. By luck I fell in with a captain of unsuspecting nature. He was a full-blooded man with a taste for rum and bent on having a good time. I managed to get myself and a number of my men invited aboard his vessel one evening, just after he was ready to sail. We made a night of it. Toward morning when his crew were about three-quarters down, we nailed them.

"I had been carrying twice as many men on my vessel as my needs required and we were able to slip both vessels out of port and turn my vessel over to the captain and his men. But they never made port. We saw to that. It has always been my unvarying policy to leave no man to come between me and long life when I have settled down ashore. Then we sailed away in *The Isabella* and gradually worked her up to what you see now —getting guns here and there, piercing her for all the guns she would carry, and making her as heavy in metal as a king's ship."

ALL this was interesting, but very disturbing. Silver had practically told me that Dykes and Monsma and I would never come to the end of this voyage alive. He would not permit us to stand in the way of his enjoying the treasure.

"We'll have as much to think about now as we can well attend to," he rattled on, paying no heed to my horror at what he had said. "The nearer we get to The Dead Man the more we shall need to watch the crew. Mark my word. It is not going to be easy to ship that treasure or to get away safely with any part of it. Naturally I have thought about that, and I have a scheme to bring my part off and put it where I can use it.

"But I'll need to keep these wolves at bay while I am doing it. You know Murray's way. Any man that balked was cut down where he stood. And Flint had his way—what a way it was! Alone with that treasure and six men of the crew, he tricked everyone. And when he got back to the ship alone—you will remember about that."

I did remember. I would never forget it! I had dreamed for years of John Flint's face as I saw it that morning. What he had been through had made him almost stark mad, but he looked about him at his crew with shrewd calculation and unutterable defiance. Billy Bones had shouldered his way forward and had asked about the six men who had gone to the island with Flint and had not returned. Flint's insane laugh had frightened every man aboard with the possible exception of Long John Silver.

"There were six stayed ashore," said Flint. "Six tall fellows. And Allardyce said he was safe wi' six!" Once more that mad laugh rang out causing every heart to quail with terror. Then he had called for rum, took it at a gulp, and began to sing in a voice as high-pitched and strange as that of gibbering ghosts:

"Tom Avery died of a cutlass slash,
Yo-ho-ho, and a bottle of rum!
Mounseer Tessin felt the galley's lash,
Yo-ho-ho, and a bottle of rum!"

Shaken as I was by what Silver had said I felt quite sure that this would not be his way. He was not as forthright as Murray, nor as headlong as Flint. That he would be as bad as both Flint and Murray together I had no reason to doubt. In addition to his utter cruelty, he was as wily as a fox and would exterminate us when we were completely helpless.

This opinion of him I soon had reason to know was correct. I caught him regarding me frequently with a cold, merciless calculation which set me trembling. I knew that when the time came unless something improbable happened, nothing more than my ghost would ever rise up to accuse him when he went back to Merrie England.

I went outside depressed, fearful Dirk was at the wheel. Lopez Silver in one of his moods of generosity had begun the task of teaching him to handle a ship. For a week now Dirk had been taking his turn at the wheel.

"Hello, Darby," he called to me. "See how well I do this! I think I'll make this a regular business. I like it. Perhaps I shall be captain of my own ship some day."

His eyes twinkled and he smiled pleasantly as he spoke.

"The very thing!" I exclaimed. "It might be a way out for—"

He placed a hand over my mouth and gave me a warning glance. "Some people use a little common sense when they talk," he remarked dryly. "And some do better without saying a word. I think you will do well to be silent since you seem to have no judgment whatever."

I smiled ruefully. After all, my hope was not well founded. Silver had his own reasons for teaching Dirk to handle the vessel. It was a part of his general policy to be looking ahead, to have a strong man ready to take the wheel when he was needed, and one who had no connection with the crew.

"Trust the Captain!" I replied finally. "It might be his way out, too. Another shot in his locker in case of need."

"Darby," began Dirk smiling at me chidingly, "sometimes you give promise of actually becoming intelligent some day. And you'd better do it as soon as you can. We shall need to do some rapid thinking to beat this man."

Dirk's words made me angry, and I easily worked myself into a fury against Silver. Why should he make any of us go along with him? Why should we pay with our lives for his comfort? Here he was using us to find the treasure and preparing to use us to bring it off safely afterward. And what would we get? Nothing but a pistol ball in our backs.

In my anger I found myself entering Silver's cabin determined to have everything made clear now while there might be some chance of saving our lives. I found him suddenly ingratiating, confidential. He asked me to sit down, declaring that he had promised to tell me a story and that now was the time. In my eagerness to hear what he had to say, I banked my fires only to have them die presently behind caution and wisdom of sober second thought.

CHAPTER XII

Flint's Treasure

"YOU would never guess where they found Billy Bones, Darby," he began. "Tucked away in England. He had picked out a cozy inn, a bit of the sea, and a hill from which he could watch the ships go by. That was his lay. But he was not a well man; and when they tackled him for Flint's map, he flew into a rage and died of apoplexy. The worst of it was, the map was not to be found. Somebody had rifled Bill's chest."

Silver took a sip of his rum and leaned back comfortably in his chair. "You'd never guess in a fortnight how it turned up," he resumed. "The first thing any one knew a country squire was out looking for foc's'le hands. He was going to look for the treasure! My father heard of him and sent a few of Flint's old crew to join on and ask questions. Sure enough, he had a map. They lost no time in getting on—Israel Hands, Job Anderson, my father, and every man of Flint's old crew left alive."

"They put to sea under a Captain Smollett," Lopez went on. "From all accounts he was a first-class man. My father regarded him very highly. He beat up to windward to get his latitude and ran down to that island as center as you could have aimed a gun. But bad luck dogged Flint's old crew from the first moment they sighted the island. Every man was for breaking loose at once and taking over—all except my father. He got all hands together ashore to smooth things out a bit and compelled every man to join up, for there were a few that did not belong to Flint's crew.

"It seems that Smollett and his crowd had caught on to the situation and were waiting for just such an event. They immediately landed with arms and ammunition and took shelter in the stockade they had sighted from the deck. My father and Flint's men tried to dislodge them but got repulsed time after time. Then the fever struck Flint's men. The schooner dragged its anchor loose and drifted away. Smollett's men found the treasure and recovered the schooner. Flint's men deposed my father. If it had not been for the fact that they captured one of Smollett's men and held him as a hostage, it would have ended with my father hanging from a yard-arm in the harbor of Liverpool."

He paused in his recital and smiled to himself as he recalled the rest of the story. "You will remember my father's mannerisms," he continued. "He had a habit of saying, 'John Silver always has another shot in his locker.' So, when everything was lost, he used his hostage to excellent advantage and joined up with Smollett again. Then they shipped the treasure and made the nearest port to get a new crew. That was my father's chance and he took it.

"While everybody was ashore, except Ben Gunn, he broke out a considerable amount of treasure, put it overside in a boat, and made his escape. That seemed much better to him than to go home dead broke, when he knew that my mother was waiting for him three thousand miles away in another city. And that's the story, McGraw—just as my father told it to me. We'll profit by some of his mistakes and keep Murray's cache for ourselves. And we'll make it. Nothing will cheat me now!"

He pronounced these last sentences in an icy tone that made me shiver. His face was cold and cruel and his eyes were like pin-points. No one could doubt that Lopez Silver was staking everything on this one throw of the dice. If necessary, he would put every man aboard to death in order to achieve his ends.

It was no great while after this that I noticed a subtle change in the crew. There was no refusing to perform their duties, nor was there any show of insolence or sullenness. The men would now and then let their eyes rove over Lopez Silver as if measuring his strength in a fight. There seemed to be less enthusiasm for him, a cool, calculating attitude whenever he approached.

I wondered at the change. I wondered also if they had ever seen Lopez Silver in action. Among so many he seemed comparatively helpless, but I felt sure that with a cutlass and standing room no two men of the crew dared to take him on. With his back to a wall he could hold his own against almost any number of these headlong wolves of the sea. He would leave a ring of their bodies to mark the spot where they pulled him down. Long John Silver would see to it that his son was given the best instruction in swordsmanship that money could procure. Even if he had learned only what his father could teach him, he would be no man to hold lightly.

I knew of course that there were desperate men aboard, men who would not hold back on account of danger. Once the word was given, and the rush began, nothing could save Lopez Silver but his sword arm and his craft. But I knew that he was ready for such an emergency, he had already told me so. He was not a man to put to sea with such men without going over every possible emergency.

Early the following Tuesday we heard a cry in the foretop, "Land ho!" We rushed forward and saw dead ahead a dark object which seemed at that distance to be about the size of a man's fist. "The Dead Man's Chest!" the crew exulted. At once I caught a glimpse of such uncontrollable greed in their faces as frightened me. Men actually licked their lips as if they could savor and taste all that gold. Calculating, suspicious glances and gleams of baleful intent went the round of this ravenous herd of filth.

SILVER came forward and leveled his glasses at the island. "Well, men," he remarked with what seemed a happy chuckle, "there lies the island. We hit it just as squarely as Smollett hit Treasure Island on his trip to dry up Flint's cache. When it comes to taking a ship somewhere, it's a wise thing to have someone on deck who can lay a course."

I saw the crew exchange glances with one another and look toward two of their number who stood a little back of Silver and to his left. These were Conrad, the coxswain, and Butler who had been acting as first mate since MacGregor had gone overside. I saw a look of confident scorn on Butler's face and just the flicker of uneasiness in Conrad's eyes.

It all happened in the fraction of a minute, and I was never able afterward to say just how it began. The first thing I knew Silver had stepped two paces backward until he stood beside Butler and Conrad. His face was wreathed in exultant smiles.

"Three cheers, bullies!" he commanded. "Three cheers for the ship and the men who will bring off the gold from the Dead Man!"

Silver had drawn his sword and was flourishing it as he led the cheer. Then suddenly there was a lightning flash of his weapon and Butler was toppling down to the deck. Another flash like the silver gleam of passing wings and Conrad had fallen beside Butler. Before the crew could recover from its surprise, Silver had stepped quickly behind his two victims and stood with the blood rivuleting down his extended sword.

"You expected to fool Lopez Silver, did you?" he taunted them. "May I observe that not one of you has enough above his shoulders to do that? There are your leaders, you bar-flies, and tramps, and scum of the ports! Look at them! Look at them and see what your fate will be unless you go along quiet. And any man not satisfied will be satisfied here and now. Come on, any one or all of you!"

The audacity of Silver, the speed with which he had struck to rob them of the two men who were to head the mutiny, and the horror of his deed, left the sailors cowed, aghast, and afraid to rush him. Fear settled on every man and there was a spontaneous protest of loyalty and much pleading for mercy.

"Going to knuckle, are you?" Silver sneered. "No taste for meeting any man that will stand up to you, have you? I knew what you were, just cowardly dirty swabs! Now get to your places, every man of you, or I'll make you walk the plank. Throw those pieces of carrion overboard and be quick about it, before I cut you down and drop you overside with them."

There was a choked and broken "Aye, aye, sir," and every man fled to his station as if the devil were at his heels. And no wonder. Silver's deed had been so deadly, so monstrous, so utterly heartless, that it amazed and crushed the boldest spirit among the crew. Each man now scuttled about deck like a fleeing rat, more than glad to get out of sight of the captain at any cost.

Silver had broken them, and he had done it with a single blow. They did not dare to meet him now, for no one of them could even guess what all he knew or where he would strike next. The more guilty ones were white with fear or shaking like a leaf in the wind.

"Bring her in close, Monsma," said Silver in a quiet voice to Dirk who had been at the wheel. "I'll give you the signal to stand to."

We slipped in under the lee of a brush-covered knoll and were about a quarter of a league off shore. A man with the lead was in the fore-chains sounding and calling back to us the depths of the waters. Silver stood by with one eye upon our goal and the other devoted to his beaten crew. "Bring her about," he called to Dirk. *The Isabella* swung broadside to The Dead Man and began to drift. "Luff!" called Silver impatiently. "Luff, you buckskin lubber!" Dirk brought her 'round nearer the wind and a flock of sailors went aloft to trim her. "Cast anchor!" shouted Silver to the capstan crew. There was a resounding splash and the *Isabella* rocked in a light swell held fast by her groaning cables.

Our position was not a safe one and could be kept only so long as the sea remained calm. There was, therefore, need of all possible haste in locating the treasure and getting it aboard. Boats were immediately lowered loaded with provisions and tools, and men were tolled off to hunt for treasure. At Silver's word the boats went ashore and the supplies were carried off. Two or three trips were made and I began to wonder what the captain was about. Did he mean to take us all with him and leave only a watch on deck?

I was not left long in perplexity. He embarked two thirds of the crew and sent them off, after which he summoned the rest to the mast.

"Men, I'm taking you just as you stand," he said. "I know you have been plotting against me. I am not such a fool as to believe that you are going to resist the next temptation. But I'll be ready for you when you try it. I'm going ashore with Dykes and McGraw and the rest of the crew to find Murray's cache. I'm leaving you with the ship. It's to your interest to stand off and to lay by. But in case you should make up your minds to leave me behind, I'll remind you of the facts. None of you can lay a course. No man can fight her if she runs into trouble. You can't make port or last without me. I trust you'll be sensible, but in case you may forget I am leaving Monsma in charge. He can whip you into a pack of whimpering dogs with his two bare hands. If you think I am needed aboard, fire the gun."

With that we went overside and rowed rapidly to the beach.

CHAPTER XIII

Through the Jungle

It surprised me that Dirk was to be left behind. I had gathered from what he had said during his fight to resist capture on the river that he alone knew where the treasure was concealed. I must have revealed how I felt, for Silver smiled his understanding.

"Dykes will be able to remember the directions on the map," he volunteered. "Monsma was throwing dust in my eyes when he said he was the only one who had seen the map. I knew what he was about as soon as I had a moment to think it over. But we had to have him also, in case he might be telling the truth. We'll try Dykes first. If he fails us, we'll prod his memory. And when we know he is not holding anything back, we'll send for Monsma. We'll get the treasure between them."

His eyes were cold and glittering like ice and his lips curled in a cruel smile which boded ill for my friends unless they gave the correct information.

"You may rest easy on that score," Dykes put in. "I know as much about the location of the treasure as any one, provided the map is correct. Our only difficulty will be with this tropical growth that covers the island. Neither Ormerod nor Corlaer said anything about it. It must have sprung up in the last few years. You will need to have patience until I can get my bearings."

"Certainly," chuckled Silver. "All we want is the treasure. As long as it is clear that you are honestly doing your best, we'll give you time. But the minute it appears that you are resorting to tricks we'll pull you in, and we'll likely be rough about it."

We went ashore, as nearly as Dykes could direct us, at the very spot where Murray had landed the treasure. We pulled the boats up and carried our supplies into the edge of the dense vegetation which made progress inland almost impossible.

"The treasure is buried off there in that direction," said Dykes after taking in his surroundings.

"You will be far more explicit than that," replied Lopez Silver. "'Off there somewhere' doesn't mean anything to us. We are here to locate the exact spot, and that is why you are here. Nothing short of that will satisfy us or be safe for you."

The two men eyed each other steadily, neither giving way before the other's searching glance.

"I agreed to guide you," Dykes said in a level tone. "My word means something to me, and I'll keep it to the letter."

Lopez Silver's lips wore a mocking smile at first, but gradually his entire countenance changed to a look of genuine respect.

"Your pardon, Dykes," he answered. "I don't encounter many honorable men in my business. I'm sure you'll do your best."

"Now that we understand each other," Dykes continued, "I wish you would help me up this tree. I'll need to take a look for the landmarks they used. These trees are at least ten feet higher than Corlaer said they were, and a dozen times as thick on the ground."

"Boost him there, you scum," ordered Silver. "We can't afford to waste time. We must act quickly, for we don't know when a ship will come along; and there is no guarantee that the weather will hold."

They promptly assisted Dykes into the lower branches of the tree and he made his way rapidly to a position where he could look off across the island. He sat studying the landscape a moment, looked down below him, and back again at the expanse of vegetation.

"Move to the left, Darby," he called to me presently. "Farther over. Now, hold your position until I get down."

I stood in my tracks and watched him slip down through the branches of the tree and reach the ground safely. He came and stood beside me.

"Now, Captain," he said, "Right on a line with Darby and the tree I climbed is the direction to take. You'll need to hack a road through heavy growth, and it won't be an easy task. Nothing seems to be as they described it except a few knolls which gave me the angles. It's lucky for us that Colonel O'Donnell was an engineer and made the locations by describing the lay of the land instead of resorting to trees. There are altogether too many trees now."

"Fall to there," commanded Silver. "We'll need a road over which to bring that treasure out. Take your cutlasses and the axes and fall to!"

WE spent the whole of the morning and the afternoon in cutting our way forward through the matted jungle. Dykes was kept aloft in a tree much of the time directing our course. The atmosphere was steaming hot under the trees where not a breath of a breeze could reach us. Silver swore and fumed and threatened as the time passed and we were still a considerable distance from the point where the cache was located.

"Lay into it there, you scum!" he would hiss at the least sign of a pause on the part of any of his men. "We must ship that treasure while we can. What did you expect? Think you could pick doubloons off the sand when you got here? You lay into that or you'll never go aboard ship again."

We pressed steadily forward and came into a low blistering hot valley about sundown. But we were still surrounded and smothered by the teeming thicket which shut out the light and the air. Dykes far up above us kept shouting directions from time to time when we threatened to get off the course. Lopez Silver stumbled about below and lacerated his men with sarcastic observations and commands. The labor was great, and the result, so far, was very discouraging. It had become clear to all of us that we could do no more than locate the treasure on this first day.

Darkness descended suddenly and we felt our way out to the shore in impenetrable murk.

"Go aboard and get lights," Silver ordered. "We can't stop on account of darkness."

"That is all very well," Dykes interrupted. "But I can't see to direct the work. I can't tell you where to go unless I can see the landmarks. That as you know is quite impossible except in daylight."

Silver let out a stream of vituperation. "How am I to know that you have not been leading us astray all day? How do I know that you are not delaying us in the hope that some vessel will come up to drive us off?"

"My dear Captain," Dykes began in a level tone, "I promised to give you the directions to the best of my ability. That I did in five minutes. The only thing to hold you back was the amount of work you were willing to do to get to the treasure."

"You need not tell me that Corlaer and O'Donnell cut a road there and buried the treasure in two days!" Silver retorted.

"How they got there is none of my business," Dykes answered. "The only matter that concerns me is getting you there."

"Then heed my words, Dykes," said Silver, hissing out his syllables menacingly, "we'll locate that treasure in two hours tomorrow, or we'll have good reason to know why. So don't do anything to delay us."

"That will depend entirely upon how fast you work," Dykes shrugged. "I've kept you on the track. I'll not shorten the distance. If you want to bully someone, you've happened upon the wrong man. Threats mean nothing whatever to me."

Silver had to swallow his wrath with as much dignity as he could muster. He stamped about for some time in the darkness and finally made up his mind to go back to the ship for the night. It nettled him to be balked thus in the presence of his men, but he could do nothing about it.

"There's one consolation," he remarked later, appearing in better mood. "It's rather unlikely that any one has carried the treasure off. With all that growth to conceal it, it's as safe there as in the Bank of England. But we'll get it out tomorrow, I give you my word for that."

CHAPTER XIV

Gold

THERE was little disturbance aboard the vessel that night for Silver had driven his men like slaves all day. Every man who had been ashore fell exhausted into his bunk and was soon fast asleep. But I could not imitate their example. I felt an ominous something in the air as if some grave event were on the way. The creak and groan of the hawser, the sway and dip of the vessel, and the low voices of men on deck kept me wide awake. I began to wonder if we would ever get out of Silver's power, and how many of us would live through the storm that was sure to break when the treasure had been shipped. What would Silver do? What would the crew attempt?

At last toward morning I fell into a troubled sleep and saw The Dead Man ringed with ships of war, and pirates rushing up and down the island in deadly conflict with their enemies. A bell was tolling dismally, and great waves, mountains high, washed over the island carrying away men and trees and the last trace of the treasure.

I awoke at last and found that it was time to breakfast and to be on our way once more to find the treasure. Silver was routing us out and hurling commands about the ship. This was the day of days. He had planned for it through ten years of danger and toil. There was a new ring in his voice—a tone suggesting power, accomplishment, indefatigable purpose.

He had us hacking away at the jungle in an hour and working rapidly to get through before the intense heat arrived.

His voice was like a sword for sharpness, and every man understood that he was in a dangerous mood. The crew fell to their tasks with a will, and we advanced with more speed than on the previous day.

About nine o'clock Dykes descended from his tree, saying, "This is the spot, if the map is correct. This is the sort of growth they scattered over the cache to conceal it. Clear a space about thirty feet square and you will be ready to use pick and shovel."

I have never seen such a change come over any man as that which now took possession of Silver. His eyes glared cruelly at us. The veins stood out upon his forehead. Treachery, cupidity, all the depths of his base and selfish soul were clearly visible. No man's life would be safe once he had the treasure between decks.

"Fall to, you swabs!" he roared, impatient beyond all power to control himself. "Fall to! Get a space clear! At it, all of you!"

But the pirates had little need for his urging. They hacked and lunged at the jungle walls like wild beasts at the bars of a cage. In a few minutes the space was clear, and a dozen men were tearing at the earth with pick and shovel. Ten minutes they toiled—twenty minutes. There was no sound except the sobbing breath of weary men who forced themselves, regardless of the great heat, to keep the tools busy. Then came a new sound—the stroke of the spade on wood and iron. A shout went up and the digging was executed with feverish zeal. An instant later, the first chest was laid bare.

The jungle rang with the excited cheers of the crew. Lopez Silver stood by, rubbing his hands together and laughing, meanwhile the tears were running down his cheeks. But as more and more chests came to light, his mood suddenly changed and he began to circle around the pit like a tiger drawing nearer to its helpless prey.

"Get it out of there!" he shouted. "Some of you hand them out while others carry them back to the shore. Get a move on there! Set it all down above high tide and come back for more. Get it going out of here!"

He did not know that he was raging like a madman. His one thought was to get all this wealth on board so that he could pull up anchor and sail away. In his excitement he was both terrible and amusing. He wanted to be everywhere at once, could not bear to let any of the treasure out of his sight. All morning long he ran from the cache to the shore and back again, cursing, urging his men on, shouting down the line a thousand unheeded directions, and often getting in the way of toiling men who pushed him aside and struggled on. Every man strained, fought, cursed, tugged until he was ready to drop, and somehow kept on in his delirium of greed. It was all like the march of fiends up the slope of hell in the toils of a curse.

It was mid-afternoon before the last chest, and the last of the bar-silver, had come to rest upon the shore. No one had eaten or even felt the want of food. Here was gold, an amount beyond the dreams of any man present. That was food enough for those who snatched at it like ravenous beasts and growled at one another over it.

They had not noticed the heat, the sudden calm, the growing gloom that settled over the island. They had only one sense that functioned—that which dwelt upon the treasure. They had but one desire and that they were now glutting to the full. They ran in and out of the jungle path like ants laden with store and all oblivious of the weather and the sky.

An eighteen boomed from the deck of *The Isabella* and a ball went moaning over the island like a lost soul. Every pirate sprang forward, cutlass in hand. No one would get their treasure from them. They would defend it with their lives. Then they saw for the first time that disturbing portent of the coming hurricane.

"God Almighty!" ejaculated Silver, awaking as one who had been walking in a dream. "It's coming on to blow, mates! Aboard ship! No, here!"

He tore open a huge chest of doubloons. "Take a handful, every man of you! We can't move this now. We can't stay here another minute. We must get aboard and save the ship or everything is lost. Hurry! Get going, or we are done for!"

Each pirate plunged at the chest and poured great handfuls of the minted gold into the breast of his shirt until not a doubloon was left.

"Man the boats!" stormed Silver, cutlass in hand and driving them down to the water's edge. At last he had accomplished the almost impossible and every man had embarked. And none too soon, for the waves had already greatly increased in height, and respectable combers went by threatening to turn the boats upside down.

Silver's boat was the last to reach *The Isabella*. He watched his men scampering up the side and hauling their boats in as quickly as they could. Now his own boat was alongside. He sent up the men with him with the exception of three whom he held back.

"Now," he said, as he put his foot on the rope ladder, "you three cut back to The Dead Man and haul that treasure high and dry. We'll ride out this storm and pick you up later. And stay out of sight. We don't want any passing ship to spy you and send a boat ashore to ask questions. Now get going, or you'll never make it."

The boat pushed off and was swept rapidly in shore, hastened by the increasing wind. Silver mounted to the deck and took command, his voice rising above the wind like a trumpet as he ordered the ship turned out to sea.

CHAPTER XV

The Hurricane

THERE was much to be done and little enough time in which to accomplish it. Men raced aloft to spread sail; the anchor was raised; and the ship was brought as near the wind as was safe in order that we might drive far enough out to let her pass the end of the island. She fought forward, inch by inch. Dirk was at the wheel and held her on her course, his great muscles rippling through his clothes in response to his effort.

"Hold her, Monsma!" gasped Lopez Silver as he watched the billows coming in with their tons of water. "Hold her, or we shall go ashore! We must get out of this!"

The waves now seemed to increase suddenly into enormous seas, as high as the ship, and the wind roared by with a force that threatened to carry every stick out of her. On and on, inch by inch, we fought our way, but the weight of water was carrying us in. Would we be able to pass the point of the island? And if we should, would there be enough depth to keep us afloat?

We would soon be able to answer that question. Yes, we would pass, just pass, if we continued at our present rate of progress. Already a cheer from the men could be heard like a far off shout in the wind. Then without warning the storm drew in its breath, leaving us becalmed and at the mercy of the giant rollers which swept us in toward shore.

A cry of dismay came instantly from the crew, for it seemed certain now that we were going to strike. Nothing could save us. I watched the nearing shore in dumb agony a moment, and then hid my face in my hands. At that instant something struck us with tremendous force and the timbers screamed with the strain put upon them. The ship seemed actually to leap forward, throwing many of us off our feet. Then we rose mountains high and seemed to careen over on our side. We came down a long distance away, and I was sure that we had foundered.

"Now, Monsma!" shouted Silver, above the roar of the storm and the wild cries of the frightened crew. "Bring her about before the wind! Bring her about, man! For God's sake bring her about!"

We seemed to be whirling in a tossing cauldron and, by the best of luck, I managed to lay hold upon the foremast where I had tumbled. I held on. The ship presently settled down to a steady weaving and pitching. I opened my eyes and saw the island astern and *The Isabella* rushing like a wild white bird before the wind.

"Monsma," said Lopez Silver, fervently, "I'll never forget this! And any time you want them, I'll give you your seaman's papers. You pulled us through, and I don't believe another man aboard could have handled her. Keep her on her course."

He did not leave Dirk's side but stood with gray drawn face watching the sky grow black until a thick gloom almost hid the foremast from view.

"This is a terrible blow, isn't it?" I choked out between my chattering teeth. The sailor whom I had addressed was pale, and he turned to regard me a moment before he replied.

"Mate, it hasn't done anything yet. But it is going to be a blow. Aye, it will be some blow, and you can lay to that!"

I stood before him dumb and sick at his words. The sailor saw my state, and since the wind, or the narrow margin of our escape, had awakened some humanity in him, his eyes seemed suddenly to grow kind.

"I wish I could help you, mate. I wish somebody could help me. We are going to need it before we get through. I rode out one of these hurricanes once, but I was lucky. And I'm afraid I used up all my luck that time."

I looked about me hopelessly. There was nothing to see but a heaving world above and below. Sky and water met and interpenetrated in one vast spectacle of motion. We were being swept forward at a terrific rate. Silver, with gray face and sick staring eyes that glittered with fear, shouted hoarse words of command into Dirk's ear. Men were coming down from the top now where they had stripped us almost to bare poles. They went weaving to their stations, fighting to keep from going overboard.

"You can't mean that it will get worse than this?" I exclaimed.

"Mate, if I was you and free to do it, I'd get into my bunk and sit tight," the pirate answered. "And I'd go while I could get there safe and sound."

My heart stood still and my body ached with fear at what he had said. And when his white face showed me that he was in dead earnest, I did not hesitate to take his advice. I found Dykes inside with his head in his hands, dumbly contemplating the horrors of his own thoughts. I sat down trembling with alarm. Everywhere I looked I encountered men who were unmistakably afraid. I dropped back upon my bunk and gave myself up for lost and waited numbly for the end to come.

There were ages and ages of noise after that. I was in a wooden shell that echoed to the beat of great thunders. We rose and fell. We were pitched forward, down and down, as if we would never fetch up again. The minutes were hours, and the hours were endless agonies. The ship groaned and screamed as if her heart were broken.

In my despair I sprang up and tried to open the cabin door to look out on deck. I succeeded only in getting a glimpse of bare poles describing an arc before my eyes. The masts seemed to rise out of the sea, to sweep toward the heavens, and back again. A great avalanche of waters came in upon me and dashed me back against the wall. I spluttered and cried out in consternation, believing that the sea had swallowed us up. I saw Dykes leap forward and close the door.

"Try to get hold of yourself, Darby," he advised in a trembling voice and resumed his staring into space.

I resigned myself now to the noise and the ceaseless motion. I was ill, and seized with insufferable terrors. I sought to call to Dykes and could only gasp. I sought to get up and found my hands motionless. I lay in the thick darkness and heard the tumult of world's falling and the boom of the splintered skies. I had not a doubt that we had come to the end of the world.

But there was to be no end apparently. We wallowed, tossed, pitched, stood on end, and turned almost completely over, only to come right side up and repeat the process with countless variations. We kept on through the night and the morning of another day. Then the wind slackened somewhat, but we drifted on, sometimes riding the tops of giant combers and sometimes threading the valleys of the deep. But I began to feel more easy, for I was told that we had run out of the path of the storm. Another day and we would have a calm sea.

By mid-afternoon we were under a sallow sky and sailing under a good weight of canvas. Dirk was relieved at the wheel and came in with drawn face and burning eyes due to the strain of the last twenty-four hours. He slumped down upon the floor of the cabin and was instantly asleep. I had been frightened by his appearance, for he looked suddenly old, almost ten years older than when I had seen him take the wheel. As for Lopez Silver, he passed me, lean and haggard, but with eyes like quenchless wells of flame. My total impression of him was that of a long naked sword unsheathed and in the hands of a master swordsman.

I had no idea where we were or that our course had been changed. I knew only that we were still afloat, that every man on board was ill from the fear and strain, and that a few of us were trying to get a little food. We were indeed a sorry lot. Our decks were still awash and were caked with brine. In every part of the ship things were tumbled in great disorder.

He was like a bronze figure, facing the elements with unbreakable will.

ALL the rest of that afternoon we drove forward under a lowering sky. The wind was always brisk, but very irregular in its direction. I saw the weather-wise gravely scanning the heavens and the sea and shaking their heads.

"Don't look good to me," said one of the men as he watched the mountain ridges of water approach and recede. "We are out of the path just now, but that hurricane is running wild. There'll be many a ship go down in this. Lucky for us we got away from the island and had plenty of sea room. There'll be many as won't have it."

The wind seemed to increase suddenly toward evening and we turned to run before it. If we were on our way back to The Dead Man, we would not require many hours to get there at this rate, I thought.

A perceptible gloom began to creep over the sea, and the giant waves were like shadows in the dim light. A man came rushing forward toward us. "The glass is going down fast!" he shouted. "Wake the Captain! We've got to do something before it breaks loose on us again!"

"God help us!" said another fervently. What was happening was a mystery to me, but to see such hard and fearless men in a panic showed me that we were in the gravest peril.

Lopez Silver appeared on deck and took his position beside the man at the wheel. He was unmistakably worried as he studied the sky and the sea. Presently he seemed to make up his mind.

"Bring her two point off the wind," he commanded. "Bear off and we may be able to get clear." He muttered something about our sailing back into the storm, but his words were lost in the increasing tumult of the wind. The man at the wheel obeyed, but it was still quite apparent to all of us that Silver was by no means sure that he had chosen the right course.

By the time darkness came, we were threading enormous seas. The course was changed a second time. The crew stood about with their eyes upon Silver, showing in their faces every emotion from stark fear to dull despair. I followed their glances from time to time, and was thus able to see Silver at the exact moment when he knew beyond all doubt what was coming. His eyes grew wide with alarm and the muscles of his face drew the flesh into grim lines.

"Here she comes!" someone cried out. I followed his glance off to starboard and saw by a flash of lightning a terrifying spectacle. The sea two leagues away seemed to be a mass of boiling foam leaping to the heavens.

Silver's voice rang out with a dozen orders. Sailors flew aloft and began to reef the sails. We were going back to bare poles again. Now we would repeat the perils and terror of the last twenty-four hours. Our hearts sank, for this time no one expected to come through alive.

I saw Dirk emerge from his cabin. To my great surprise he seemed almost completely restored, although I felt sure that his excitement had much to do with his refreshed appearance. He was munching some sort of food and was calling between each mouthful a bantering sally to the crew about him. He went toward the wheel, casting level glances as he went, at the tumbling, mountainous waters. It dawned upon me then that Silver had sent for him to take over. I hurried toward him as rapidly as I could in the driving wind.

"To the wheel, Monsma," said Silver, "I think we are in for another blow. Get the feel of her before the storm breaks. That is the trouble with hurricanes, you run out of them and they circle back to hit you a second time. After it breaks, we may be able to escape. We could be sure of it if we knew which way to turn."

Without a word, Dirk grasped the wheel. He held stolidly, the muscles of his jaw bulging, and his great arms tense. He soon got the feel of the ship and settled down like a perfect and inexhaustible machine. The waves appeared to increase in height, and the wind came on in increasing gusts of ever louder tone. We were indeed back in the storm. Silver's eyes ran the length of his ship and dwelt upon the masts that seemed almost to swing over into the flying foam. He reminded me of nothing so much as a bronze figure facing the elements with unbreakable will.

I slipped back to our cabin, impressed with the quality of the two men who held our fate in their hands. Dirk would go on and on as long as the wheel remained above water. And Lopez Silver was supported by a dream of magnificence for which he had given years of his life. As long as the ship held together, these men would remain where they were, performing superhuman tasks. What I had seen heartened me, and I found myself exulting in their strength and almost welcoming each increase of the thunders of wind and water.

"They cannot be beaten," I kept telling myself. "They'll not fail. They are unbreakable. They will be there when the storm beats out its wrath and there is no port left for us to make."

We had two days of it this time—days of endless and impenetrable roaring—an incessant cannonading of waters which struck the side of the vessel and deluged the deck. Hour on hour, we leaped skyward and subsided apparently to the very bottom of the sea. We writhed and twisted forever and ever. The groaning and creaking of the great timbers of the vessel filled our ears until we felt sure that we were breaking up—being literally torn apart in every seam and joint. Yet we held.

There was no talking in all this unvarying thunder of the sea. I sat staring at Dykes who was exhausted from loss of sleep and the lack of food. His eyes were now luminous with the light of his dancing, feverish thoughts, and great dark shapes went by these lighted lamps within his mind.

We were too weary to know when the wind abated. We suddenly saw that we were threading the mountain ranges of watery hemispheres under a stiff breeze, and that so far all was well. Then just as suddenly, we were in water that would not swamp a small boat. Dirk staggered into his cabin, and it was quite clear that this time the strain had taken something from him that could never be restored.

"Dirk!" I cried in sympathy, going toward him and stopping when I saw that he was practically unaware of my presence.

"I held her up and up," he muttered. "I held her until she came through the storm." He stretched himself flat upon his bunk and continued, "I kept her nose straight. I made her jump the mountains. She came through—came through—"

Exhaustion took hold of him now and quenched his delirium in sleep. Silver came staggering in with a noggin of rum for him.

"Give him this, Darby."

"He is asleep," I protested.

Silver looked at him incredulously an instant and turned toward the door. "That man is not human," he asserted. "Seventy-eight hours at the wheel and only four hours out for a rest. He is not human. It can't be done."

CHAPTER XVI

A Sail!

THE clouds thinned, and the sun peeped through for short intervals. Lopez Silver promptly took observations, had the ship brought about on a new course, and we were soon swinging along under a great press of sail. The wind veered, rose to a brisk gale which sent us before it, groaning and creaking. Silver ordered more canvas spread and the sailors looked at him, puzzled and a little apprehensive.

"Come on," one of the pirates urged another, "you got the order, didn't you? Up with you!"

"I'm not holding back," came the reply. "But I ain't one who cares to go overboard along with the sticks. Do you suppose the hurricane left the Captain daft?"

"Maybe it's us," said the first man. "I was summat excited myself, and I don't mind saying so."

"It might be, but at least we can see the folly of what we are doing."

"It only proves that we are bound for The Dead Man. And that we are going in a hurry."

"And I'm for that, same as everyone else. But I don't aim to dive into that water if I can help it."

Two days later we sighted The Dead Man at dawn. We sailed off and on, and came later into the lee of the island, and dropped anchor in our earlier position. There were the three men we had left, eagerly waving to us, and dancing up and down in delight. They put off in their boat and were soon on board. They were ravenously hungry, for the greater part of their supplies had been carried into the sea, while they had been hauling the treasure back to a safe distance. They devoured great quantities of food while asking and answering questions. They had saved the treasure and had waited, finally giving us up for lost.

"And when we did not return in two days you buried the treasure," Silver commented. "You decided to hail the next ship that came along."

"How did you know?" exclaimed the three.

"Just what I would have done." Silver smiled indulgently.

The men finished their meal and all hands turned out to get the treasure aboard. Silver looked out at the island greedily as he ordered the boats lowered and all hands to stand by. The selection of those who were to go absorbed the attention of every man, for there was not one of us who did not want to make the trip.

As fast as men were tolled off, they went overside into the boats and shoved off with a great shouting and splashing of oars. Lopez Silver seemed to take a wicked delight in holding back the most impatient men and keeping them for his boat. Meanwhile, a number of the other boats had departed and the foremost was half way to shore.

Silver with a mocking grin turned to give a final word of instruction to those who were to remain with the ship. I was watching him closely and saw his mouth open wide in astonishment and his brows go black with rage.

"A sail!" he cried. "Coming on to starboard! And not a man to see it! You filth of all the fever-holes of the world, where were your eyes?"

He blew a whistle to recall his men who were rapidly pushing on to the island. Some heard him and turned back, but others continued to shout and swing their oars at a great rate.

"Fire that gun!" shouted Silver. "Get them back here! That is no friendly sail, and I don't like the way she acts."

By the time two boatloads had come overside it was apparent that we could wait no longer. Friend or enemy we must stand out to sea. The anchor came up, a man took the wheel, and sail was spread. The wind caught us and we were under way when a shot from the oncoming ship passed across our bow.

Silver's eyes glittered with wrath. "At her there, Cowden!" he called. "Give her as good as she sends."

ONE of the eighteens on our deck thundered. A moment later it was evident that Cowden had given a little better than we had received, for his shot had raked the deck on the enemy vessel and had produced no little confusion there. Two shots came at once from the other ship but they were not aimed at us. We looked back and saw our abandoned boats thrown bodily out of the water to dissolve in splinters. At least a third of our crew had been wiped out, and among them the three men who had hidden the treasure.

Silver's wrath mounted at the sight. He shook his fist, lifting it high above his head. "Now, I swear that I shall sink you! Lay them right down on her, Cowden! Do all the damage you can!"

The gunner went to work and a second time the eighteens found their mark. We could not see the amount of damage from our deck, but it was sufficient to cause our antagonist to veer off a point as if seeking to avoid us.

"Don't like them, do you?" sneered Lopez Silver. "And you have only begun to take them."

He ordered the ship brought a point nearer the enemy, and we were now racing away from the island on approximately parallel courses and popping away at each other in real earnest. Twice our enemy reached us, one shot silencing one of our eighteens, throwing the mangled bodies of two men about the deck. Ben Gunn was one of these. He had died a pirate and in action as he would have preferred.

"Over another point," said Silver to the man at the wheel. "We'll make her sorry for that."

Dirk ran to the overturned gun and strained at it to set it up in its place. To our amazement he nearly succeeded. A dozen men with bars hastened to lend a hand and tugged and pulled until the gun was set upright and pushed into place. A new crew took it over with a shout and soon had it alternating in rhythm with its mate.

"Monsma, you are worth your salt!" exulted Silver after seeing how Dirk had directed the men in putting the gun back into action. "Without you we might have been lost in the storm, and now you've put us back on even terms with that scoundrel out there."

We settled down now to a long, determined chase which occupied the rest of the day. We were driving northward, each captain trying for an advantage, and each afraid to venture too near the other, lest he come to disaster. Occasionally each tried a long range shot in the hope of doing enough damage to cripple the other vessel. Nothing of the sort happened, and we held on through the evening and the night, bearing always a little toward the east.

"He is pulling away from the track of king's ships, and that suits me in every way," chuckled Silver. "Now we'll lay her by the heels. *We'll teach her people to* fire on us. This is their last voyage."

It was a cloudless night with a fine moon to give us light, and we kept the enemy in view. Once, while the moon loitered behind a cloud toward morning, she tried to give us the slip. She quickly altered her course and slipped away on the backward course. But she could not elude Lopez Silver.

"That was the game all the time," he laughed. "Well, it didn't work. She'll haul to and fight before the day is over. We have her nailed, and at least one rover has come to the end of his course."

He crowded on more sail now, and still more, for he was bent on coming up with her. Heretofore we had been chased and had then given chase; now we took over the role of destroyer. By daylight it was apparent that we had shortened the distance appreciably and that in another hour we would be ready to strike. All hands stood by ready to board her when the time came, for it was now clear that Silver meant to engage her hand to hand.

We continued to draw up, and some half an hour later, Cowden began to lay his shots down upon the enemy's deck again. We were also getting our share of trouble in return, but our vessel was in no way greatly damaged, and we held on. We raked her deck; nicked one of her masts, causing it to lean perilously; and swept always nearer as the moments passed. Another crash from our eighteens some time later clipped the mizzen-mast and sent down royal and top-gallants to drift outward like the broken wing of a bird.

"Now, my fine fellow!" hissed Silver's cold revengeful voice. "I've got you! Give her everything you have, Cowden!"

We drew near enough and in position to give her a full broadside and to take a part of hers in the reply. We went about with our whole gun-deck in commotion. There were screams and curses of wounded men. We turned and blasted her with the other side, this time with more damaging effect than we had wrought hitherto. She was now practically helpless and could have been pounded to pieces where she stood, had Silver desired to do so. He had, however, another purpose in mind and sent his vessel about, to get in a position where he could draw alongside and board her.

"Drowning is quite too good for them," he remarked. "They are going to walk the plank if any of them are left alive after the ship is taken. We'll board and see how they like the cutlass and the pistol. Come on, bullies. They sank your mates when they were helpless. We'll return the favor."

A wild blood-curdling shout from the crew answered him. Cowden who had stuck to his guns had made a shambles of the enemy's deck by the time we sent the grappling irons home. As soon as we touched, half of our crew swarmed over to engage her men on their own deck. It was a merciless affair. They hacked and hewed and screamed and went down with shouts of defiance. Red and green and scarlet kerchiefs were bobbing swiftly before my eyes. Men roared like beasts as they sprang for one another. The whole scene was a jumble of flashing cutlasses and swaying color growing more thin and closing up to leave the deck strewn with the writhing and quiet figures of the dying. Not many of our men would survive the slaughter on that bitterly defended deck.

Then to our amazement the scene seemed once more crowded with the crew of the enemy and our men were being hurled back just at what had appeared to be the moment of victory. We had been outnumbered from the first, but now the odds seemed all against us. Beside this, the two ships had been firmly lashed together and we could not possibly draw off. It was now win or lose just as we were. Our men came scurrying back to their own ship, closely followed by the enemy.

"At them, men! Down with them, bullies!" cried Silver, laying about vigorously with his cutlass.

CHAPTER XVII

MacGregor Again

It was our turn to be on the defensive now. On and on rushed our enemies, coming over by the dozens with dirks between their teeth, their cutlasses driving everything before them. We let them surge by and fell upon their exposed flanks. Dykes and I were close together and fighting because we must. We wounded our assailants, causing them to flee. We had time for a glance about us and saw that our men were giving a good account of themselves. Silver, single-handed, was keeping a space clear by the deadliness of his lightning thrusts. Then I gasped, for I caught sight of MacGregor coming over! He dropped upon our deck and went bellowing to meet Silver.

"Silver, laddie," he mocked. "You ken what I told ye? I cam to hae it oot wi' ye, mon! And ye look tasked. Are ye no feeling braw the noo? Ah weel, I was no feelin' sae good mesel' when ye dropped me overside. But this time ye'll no be shootin' at me back. I gie ye my word for that, mon."

With that he began to circle about to get near enough to engage Silver and to avoid running into anyone else. It was at this moment that I saw Dirk for the first time during the fight. He walked up behind MacGregor and struck his arm a smart blow, causing him to drop his cutlass. MacGregor turned upon him with his dirk, only to find his hand firmly held as in a vise.

Dykes and I had a good view of the struggle, for we were blocked off by them from the rest of the ship. A dozen times the Scot almost impaled him but always the weapon was turned aside. They swayed back and forth, up and down their part of the deck, straining, emitting great sobs in breathing, and both purple from the intensity of their effort. Just beyond, we could see the flash of gleaming cutlasses and hear the cries of the other contestants.

Dykes and I moved a little to one side, thinking that we might be able to slip by and engage some of the enemy, but we were not to do so. MacGregor rushed Dirk backward, flush against the rail. He had wounded Dirk slightly and now hoped to make a speedy end of the fight. They struggled a moment like two great bulls,

MacGregor trying to bend Dirk backward and over the rail.

Then I saw Monsma gradually slip down as if to escape being pushed overboard. One arm grasped MacGregor around the thigh and through the crotch. Slowly he drew himself up, lifting MacGregor as he rose and being careful to keep a firm hold upon the hand that held the dirk.

I did not see how this could better Monsma's chances, but I had not counted upon his slyness and his enormous strength. Suddenly he was almost erect upon his well-braced feet. Then I saw MacGregor's eyes stand wide with terror. Monsma had lifted him from the deck, slowly, higher and higher, with a sure motion that nothing could halt.

"Dinna ye do it, mon!" cried MacGregor, dropping his weapon and clutching wildly to save himself.

But he had waited too long. With a quick twist of his body, Monsma hurled him overboard, holding him so that he went down flat upon the water with a resounding smack. I looked over and saw him strike. His huge body seemed to spread out like dough upon the water's surface. A moment he lay stunned and helpless. I looked away, horrified, and when I looked back a little later nothing could be seen of MacGregor.

It was a gruesome sight which met our eyes when we turned to look over our deck. Lopez Silver had just cut down the last man opposed to him. Aside from eight men of our own crew, there seemed to be no survivors. Our deck was strewn with dead and wounded men who lay in puddles of their own blood. I saw Silver look about him, puzzled. He waited a moment, blew his whistle, and only five or six wounded men raised themselves upon their elbows to unite with the eight others in responding to his summons. Silver stood with features contorted with rage.

"The greedy swabs!" he hissed. "Leave me here to fight for my life while they plunder the other vessel. I'll break them on the triangles for this."

HE blew his whistle a second time, and more insistently than before. Again only the half dozen wounded and the eight at his side replied. Silver seemed to have another thought at that moment and it caused him to look like a cornered beast. Fear was in his eyes, and all his cunning came to the surface.

He sent men about the ship to round up the loiterers, but they returned and reported no one in sight. Sure now that there was no enemy at his back, he took his men and made a search of the enemy vessel which it appeared we had captured. He only found two men still alive and both were severely wounded. He had them carried aboard *The Isabella*. Outside of such of the wounded as might recover, there were but twelve of us left to handle the ship.

We now learned that the vessel which had attacked us was *The Bristol*. Her crew had overpowered her captain and put to sea under John Silver's old shipmate, Black Dog. It had taken them a year to accumulate guns and to make her into a first-class fighting craft. Then they had sailed out to scour the seas and to grow rich on the fat prizes that had come their way.

In a Spanish port, Black Dog had been recognized and fired upon from ambush. The wound he had received had been serious and they had carried him aboard and put to sea rather than let him fall into the hands of the authorities. They had given him attention aboard, but the wound would not heal, and he had gradually grown weaker. They had put in at Bermuda to get proper medical care for him. There they had met MacGregor and had recognized him as one of the Brotherhood. He was able to further their quest and to secure a good surgeon. But it was too late; after lingering for a few days, Black Dog had died.

MacGregor then told the crew of the hidden treasure on The Dead Man's Chest and that we were on the way to get it. He asked their help in thwarting us. They had elected him captain and had set sail at once. The storm had blown them somewhat out of their course, but the delay had not been great. It appeared that they had not encountered very much of the hurricane's wrath and so had been able to use the time we had lost.

"That comes of being sentimental," said Silver scornfully. "And that is the usual result of a kindness shown to ungrateful scum."

"That comes of missing him and giving him only a bad wound," laughed Dirk.

"When one makes up his mind it is time to shoot, he ought to shoot straight."

Silver's eyes were a study. Surprise, craft, cruelty, and wicked resolve glittered there. Then he looked away quickly and let his glance rove about the two ships.

"However we view it," he resumed at last, "it was unfortunate. Here we are with almost no one to man the ship."

"And that comes of not taking the safe way of meeting the enemy," said Dirk, determined to badger Silver as much as he dared.

"Arguing helps none at all." Silver shrugged, indicating that so far as he was concerned, the matter was closed. "Fall to and dress the wounds of those left alive. With the few that we can pull through we must be satisfied. We'll be short-handed, but it can't be helped."

He turned now to go aboard *The Bristol*, and we hastened to minister to the unfortunates who groaned and begged for our help. We carried them below and did what we could to make them comfortable.

CHAPTER XVIII

"We've Been Tricked!"

An hour later Silver had completed his investigations on board *The Bristol* and had returned to look after the effects of such men of *The Isabella* as had perished in the battle. He carried everything to his cabin, saying that he would go through the lot later and make such disposition as seemed best to him. This done he went back to *The Bristol* where he remained some time.

Later he came to the rail of the captured ship and commanded us to take up the grapnels and to stand off at a safe distance to wait for him. This we did, and some twenty minutes later we saw him slide down a rope and into a boat. He was not long in reaching *The Isabella* and in coming on board.

"Let her go, Monsma; south by west ought to do well enough," he ordered briefly and turned to let his eyes rest upon the ship we were rapidly leaving astern. We heard a splintering noise like thunder. *The Bristol* rocked, fell apart, and smoke burst from her sides in a dozen places. She shuddered, a mangled, riven thing, and sank almost at once.

"And that is that," observed Silver, half to himself. "Keep us on the course, Monsma. We'll be short-handed the rest of the way, and it will not be an easy task to get the treasure aboard, but given time enough, we ought to manage. Our first task will be to find where the men buried it, but that ought not to take a great while. In any case, we may be sure they never carried it far. We'll dig around until we hit upon a soft spot of earth. That will be the end of the search."

He went now to his cabin, ostensibly to go through the sea-chests and bags of the men we had lost.

"He has things about as he wants them now," said Dirk when we were alone. "There's not enough men to carry out a mutiny, and that makes him safe and puts more in his pocket. It has been a long shot for him, but with luck he'll pull through. A few more lucky accidents and he'll be home in Parliament and the stoutest defender of maritime law in the kingdom."

We drove before the wind all that day and the following night, making such good time that we were scanning the horizon at daybreak for a sight of The Dead Man. Three hours later the island swam into view a little to starboard. We drew up under the lee of the shore for the third time and without a moment's delay made our preparations to bring the treasure off.

Two or three of the wounded men were now able to hobble on deck to see Dykes, Silver, and I paddled out to the island. Dirk was left in charge of the ship. He was to keep a sharp lookout for any craft that might seek to approach. Cowden managed to limp over to the guns and get one of them ready to fire in case a shot should be needed to call us on board. We were quite cheerful as we reached the land. It would take no little time to dig up the treasure and transport it to the ship, but we knew that we could do it.

Delay was what we most dreaded, and it began the moment we started out to make our locations. The Dead Man had been drenched and packed by heavy rains. The path we had hacked into the jungle had begun to fill up with the rapidly growing vegetation. In another month no one would be able to see that our runway had been cut through the tangled mass. We examined the earth closely, being careful also to inspect the shrubs and trees to see if any of them had been transplanted. It was a tedious labor and consumed much time.

Silver naturally grew impatient as the time passed and declared that we must find the treasure soon. We could not keep the ship standing there in plain sight of any passing vessel without provoking curiosity and a possible investigation. And just now we were in no condition to meet with unfriendly visitors.

But in spite of the wisdom of his observations, a wisdom that was all too clear to both Dykes and myself, the treasure would not come to light. After three hours of fruitless seeking, Silver's face had become sickly white. His rage waited only a sufficient opportunity to expend itself upon us. But neither his anger nor our redoubled efforts could avail anything. The gold simply could not be found.

"Hurry, you buckskin lubbers," he said impatiently. "We must find it and get it going out of here. Spread out and use your wits."

We obeyed him, spread out, drew in, recovered the ground again and again, but always with the same result. The whole morning passed; the afternoon waned; and the short twilight, before the tropical blackness came to obscure the sea and the ship, found us paddling back silent and defeated to go aboard for the night. I had never seen Silver in such an ugly mood. His chagrin made him waspish and highly dangerous. You may be sure we were very careful to say nothing to draw his wrath.

Cowden met us as we came overside. He was apparently much recovered, for he showed just enough interest to indicate that he expected to have a share in the treasure when a division was made. He was much surprised, and showed just a trace of doubt, when he heard the story of our day's activity. It was then that I knew how dangerous delay could be from another angle. A suspicious crew might take matters into its own hands and count us out of the enterprise.

"You say you can't find it, Captain Silver, sir?" he asked. "That *is* strange. You've been out there long enough to dig over most of the island I should think. There's not much hiding room out there to judge from this distance. You ought to take someone out there with sharp eyes."

"A very good suggestion, Cowden," said Silver quietly. "We'll take Monsma tomorrow. You remember that he trailed us like a dog when we carried Dykes off through the woods that time. He ought to be able to track that treasure down in no time. Thanks for the help."

THERE was something in Silver's tone that might have warned Cowden had he not been so taken up with his suspicions. But failing to hear just how Silver had spoken, he plunged dangerously on.

"And if he fails, I think we all ought to try it. Give every man a chance at it, I say. We don't have anything in particular to do except look for it. So give every man his chance, I say."

"What you say might prove very unhealthy under certain circumstances, Cowden," Silver answered in a purring silky tone. "Men have said too much aboard this ship before. They are not here now."

The quietness of Silver's words and the silence that followed them held Cowden dumb with fear.

"I—I just wanted to be of help," Cowden managed to answer, and instantly beads of sweat appeared upon his brow.

"Then see that you are not misunderstood," Silver advised. "A misunderstanding has caused no end of trouble before this. Meanwhile I'll do the planning, and the worrying as well. We'll bring that treasure out tomorrow or know the reason why. You can all lay to that."

Silver's tone of dangerous vexation convinced Cowden. His mouth and eyes opened wide with amazement.

"Captain Silver, sir," he cried out. "You've been tricked! We've all been tricked! The swabs we left behind during the storm have shipped the treasure aboard *The Bristol* and then got double-crossed themselves!"

"Not a chance, Cowden," asserted Silver, chuckling. "I admit that it could have been done. That is why we never let *The Bristol* out of our sight for a minute. And that is why we didn't stand off and send her to the bottom without boarding her, Monsma. We had to look before we sent her to the bottom. The three men we left didn't do it that way. I went all over *The Bristol*. There wasn't enough money on her to buy kerchiefs for a dozen men.

"So you see you are about four days late with your opinions, Cowden. I thought of that the moment *The Bristol* fired on our boats. I thought they were covering up their tracks and I meant to take a look aboard to see. And I looked. I opened every box and chest. I pried open every bulwark and scraped her clean. It wasn't there. And it *is* on The Dead Man. You have also been silly enough to imagine that I have gone to all this trouble just to dig up that treasure and bury it again. I saw it in your eyes the moment we came aboard tonight. But you'll think better of that tomorrow. One trip out here will be enough for me. And if I find you indulging any more distrustful fancies, this voyage will be your last."

Cowden was sorely frightened by the accuracy with which Silver had read his thoughts. He fell back, half expecting to be struck down, and began to make excuses.

"You must admit, Captain, that it looked queer," he stammered. "And you say yourself that you suspected them swabs. It's only human to think of such things and wonder where the treasure is since you didn't find it."

"I haven't seen it, Cowden; but I'm going to see it. I've spent no little time laying plans to get it, and nothing will stop me now that I know it is here."

He turned and strode quietly to his cabin, leaving us to wonder at him. How quickly he had suspected treachery when *The Bristol* first appeared! Any other man would have been caught helpless, but Silver had acted instantly to recall his scattered crew. When *The Bristol* had fired on his boats, his worst fears were confirmed. Treachery, greed, the double-cross—all were in that shot at the defenceless boats.

But there had not been a word of this to any man aboard *The Isabella*. Silver had gone about the deadly business of verifying his suspicions at no matter what cost. He was no man to fly into a panic and overlook any essential matter.

One thing at least was clear. The treasure was still on the island and we had only to dig about until it came to light. We had missed it so far, but sooner or later it would be found.

CHAPTER XIX

The Search Continues

WE were on the island by daybreak the next morning and had resumed our search. Silver looked as if he had not slept and was still in an ugly mood, suspicious, irritable, and determined.

"Track it down, Monsma," he commanded. "You can follow a trail in the dark, I know, and the rains we've had ought not to hold you up a great while. And hurry. We must get the treasure out of here today."

Dirk examined the earth carefully, slipped into the jungle and wormed his way along until he was out of sight. He was perfectly at home in the thick growth and moved noiselessly along. He made his way down one side of the path, rounded the original cache and came back on the other side of the path to the shore. He had been gone so long that we were beginning to wonder what was keeping him when he sprang out lightly from the screen of leaves to stand beside us.

"Not a sign of it so far," he replied to our questioning glances. "They have not carried it off the path into the woods on either side. It begins to appear that they used the boat and hid it at some other spot."

"The very thing," laughed Silver. "Monsma, this whole venture would have been lost at least three times without you. I'm glad we decided we had to have you along. Of course that is what has been done. We might have known it at once. They would not dare to tuck it away here where their tracks would show some visiting ship where to look. And when we stayed away and they decided to hail some passing vessel, they put it where no investigation would uncover it. Come along! Look in the growth for their tracks, Monsma, and we'll cover the shore as we go along."

We tramped down the island a considerable distance, leaving Dirk to investigate the growth a little way back from the water. We saw no sign on the shingle or the nearby sward to indicate that any human feet had ever walked there. Silver scowled, showed his great disappointment, and a little later hailed Dirk.

"Come on out, Monsma. No use sailing any farther on this tack. They would not come this far. We'll try on the other side of the path for awhile."

We trudged back in the blistering heat and ate our lunch silently. Silver's face had grown strangely dark and angry, and his eyes darted over us occasionally like those of a venomous snake. A little more fearful than ever, we rose and resumed our search.

Two hours later Dirk was called out to the shingle and questioned. Silver was very suspicious, but Dirk's frank answers showed every one that he was concealing nothing.

"You are quite sure no one has been out there?" Silver asked.

"No one has ever been out there," Dirk answered. "Not a stick or a plant has ever been disturbed. I am quite certain."

"Well, we'll go around the whole island. It looks as if those swabs did deceive us, after all. MacGregor came along and they went over to him. He took the treasure and buried it and lay concealed to wait for us. When he saw our men scamper back aboard, he realized he would have a fight of it. He sank those scoundrels so they could not tell me where it was in case he lost. But we'll raise it yet!"

We walked along more rapidly now and Dirk had hard work to keep up with us. At times we had to wait for him. We circled the island finally and came back to our boats and the path that led into the jungle. Dirk came out thoughtfully and joined us. He was very sure that no one had gone ashore at any point in the dense growth.

Lopez Silver was at that moment a very dangerous man. "You mean to tell me that the treasure is not out there somewhere?" he demanded.

"How could it be?" asked Monsma with an indifferent shrug.

"You answer my question," snarled Silver drawing his cutlass.

To the surprise of every one present Dirk's hand moved fast as light and drew from within his shirt a loaded pistol which he leveled at Silver.

"I will shoot you like a thief," he affirmed, his small blue eyes snapping with determination. "I saw no tracks out there, and no sign of your treasure. Now you have just one minute to put that cutlass where it belongs."

Lopez Silver was an excellent judge of the temper and character of men. He knew that Dirk had told him the truth and that now the pistol would be fired in just one minute. Futhermore, he knew when he was beaten. He complied with Dirk's demand.

"You are right, Monsma," he admitted promptly. "I have gone too far." He paused a moment considering. "Oh well, we are all disappointed and weary and out of humor. Let's go aboard and give it up for today."

It no doubt cost Silver a great deal to say this, but it was the only way out and he knew it. He did not wait to hear what Monsma might say, but turned to the boat and stepped in, taking his place in the stern. Dirk and I followed. I took the oars, for I knew that Dirk would give Silver no opportunity to turn the tables upon him. We did not speak until we were once more aboard *The Isabella.*

"We'll try it again tomorrow," said Silver as he walked calmly toward his cabin.

We made our way to the galley and were met by Cowden. "You'll find a bit to eat ready for you," he volunteered. "What news?"

"Not a trace of it yet," I answered.

"I reckoned you hadn't," said Cowden with a knowing smile. "I was watching you through a pair of glasses and saw that you were not getting along very well together. I guessed that Silver was threatening you when I saw Monsma level his pistol. That was a business you'll likely be sorry for. Silver is certain not to let it pass."

"If he is wise he will," Dirk answered coldly.

"He is not a man you can trust exactly," Cowden went on reflectively. "It might be a good thing to drop him overside and take a look for the treasure without him. We could—"

"No!" said Dirk heatedly. "I have no interest in this except the safety of myself and that of my friends. We've known where that treasure was hidden for at least ten years. We let it stay, and so far as I am concerned, it can stay where it is now, wherever that is. I have only one purpose—to get through this alive and get home safely."

"Thank you, Monsma," said Silver's clear icy voice. He had come up unheard and was now covering us with a pistol. "When I am through looking for the treasure we shall all go home. But I'm not through. As for you, Cowden, you'll go along tomorrow to help us look. Barby, get Monsma's pistol and hand it to me."

DIRK went on eating and never so much as lifted his eyes. Cowden turned white and seemed ready to faint. I handed over to Silver our only weapon of defence.

"It seems, Monsma, that you are not devoid of honor," Silver resumed. "And for your comfort I'll admit that I made your action justifiable. But I am not a sentimentalist, and I am here to get that treasure. Your getting home safely will depend entirely upon my success in this one undertaking. I heard what you said to this sneaking gunner, Tom Cowden. That will make a difference, but only if I get the treasure. We'll continue to look for it until we find it. As for you, Tom Cowden, I have grown very weary of your company, and both my pistols are loaded."

Cowden quailed before him and trembled violently, seeing that his life hung by a thread, and knowing that he would very probably not return from the island tomorrow. Silver calmly sat down and began to eat ravenously, keeping his eyes upon us as he did so.

"Now, I'll explain a few things if you don't mind," he said, between each mouthful of food. "There's gold enough for all of us out there. When I signed this crew, I agreed to take one-fourth and to give the crew three-fourths. We have lost at least four-fifths of the crew since those papers were signed. Most captains would declare a new basis of division under the circumstances, and you know that that is quite the usual thing among men of my trade. It is my intention to hold to my terms and to the one-fourth. I think some changes ought to be made with reference to the crew. The prisoners ought to share alike with the men in the other three-fourths. They've done as much as any one else to see us through so far, and they'll no doubt continue to be useful."

Cowden grasped instantly at this straw of hope. He had come to feel that he would not live to see the division of the treasure, and Silver's words held out an intimation that he might.

"Suits me, Captain Silver, sir," he agreed heartily. "There's no call to go grasping greedy at that gold when every man aboard will be sure to get enough for the rest of his life."

"You see it at last, do you?" asked Silver. "You are very sensible on second thought. I take it you have repented of the desire to drop me overside?"

Silver's words were cold and crisp and mocking. His lips were curved in a sneer and his eyes were beady black flashes of venom. Cowden shrank back from him and became as white as a dead man. He saw now that Silver was neither forgetting nor forgiving anything.

A moment they stared at each other, then Silver shrugged. "Well, we'll dig it up tomorrow, won't we, Monsma?"

Dirk looked at the table thoughtfully before replying. "We can dig," he answered, "but there's no getting the treasure unless we dig where it is."

"Tomorrow," said Silver, his voice sharp as a sword blade, "we'll dig where it is. It is my intention to bring that treasure aboard or to come back alone to the ship. You will have the right to think that over, and if you think wisely, I believe you will decide that it will be best to locate the treasure without any further delay."

He stepped out of the galley, leaving us breathless with the horror of what he proposed to do. We stared at Dirk and were greatly surprised at his calm.

"Well, he means that," Dirk asserted with a great shrug. "The treasure hunt is drawing to a close."

CHAPTER XX

The Tables Are Turned

THERE was no sleep for me that night. I lay in my bunk and listened enviously to Dirk's snoring, wondering how he could be so calm when he had every reason to believe that this venture would end in blood within a few hours. Dykes lay immovable in his bunk, and I could not even hear his breathing. The night was as bright as day under a full moon, and a breeze sang in the shrouds as the ship rocked in a gentle swell. And yet, in spite of the peacefulness and beauty of the night, I was deeply disturbed. Forebodings and oppressive fancies ran through my head and gnawed at my already raw nerves.

I had about made up my mind that I could endure my bed no longer when I heard a slight stir from Dykes. He was rising stealthily from his bunk. It was coming on to daylight, and already one could distinguish objects quite clearly in the cabin. He came to me and whispered, "You have not slept, Darby, nor have I. But do not be too greatly disturbed. I have a plan, and if it works we'll cheat Lopez Silver yet. Keep inside until I return, and say nothing to Dirk about my going. I'll be back before the Captain is abroad I think."

He dressed and slipped out quietly going in the direction of the foc's'le. He remained away so long that I fell into troubled sleep and did not hear him when he returned. I awoke to find the sun coming in at the port, and Dykes sitting on the side of his bunk, yawning and flexing his arms. He smiled at me reassuringly.

"All fixed to go, Darby. Go along as if you expected nothing whatever to happen. That will keep Silver confident that he has the whip hand and will help us to work our scheme. If we succeed in pulling it off, we'll give him quite a scare, and we'll get through alive."

Naturally I was expecting the scheme to be worked at the earliest possible moment, but we breakfasted and nothing happened. The boat was lowered and still there was no move from Dykes to show that any plan for our deliverance was under way. Cowden, Dirk and I went overside and took our places in the boat. Silver followed us, calling back directions to Dykes, who stood smiling and wishing us all good luck. Still nothing had happened, and we were on our way to the island to fail and to be slaughtered by an enraged Lopez Silver. Cowden was at the oars and pulled us away from the ship with a steady sweep. My heart sank within me and hopelessness dulled my sight or I should have noted that Cowden was keeping his gaze fixed upon some point in our rear. I came to the realization that something was on foot when I saw Cowden smile and nod his head vigorously.

Before I could look back to the ship to discover who was receiving his signal, there was a tremendous roar and we were thrown high into the air, to come down strangling and spluttering in the boiling waters. I could not imagine what had happened, but leaped to the conclusion that *The Isabella* had had her magazine fired. As I came to the surface, strong hands grasped me and dragged me back toward the ship. I shook the water from my eyes and saw Tom Cowden well ahead of us and Silver behind, thrashing the water and calling to us to help him with the boat. Almost at the same instant I saw Dykes standing on deck with a leveled musket which was aimed at a point behind me.

"Now, Lopez Silver," he called, "get in that boat and bring to. A suspicious move from you and I'll fire."

We could hear Silver arguing, but we did not pause in our swimming to learn the drift of what he said. We rounded the ship and came to a ladder waiting for us. Tom Cowden raced up the side as swiftly as a monkey and Dirk and I followed with all possible speed. We were all soon on deck listening to the parley between Dykes and Silver.

"All done so far, Captain Dykes," said Cowden.

DYKES expressed his thanks in a word, but kept his eyes riveted upon Silver. It was now clear to me what had happened. Cowden had loaded and trained the gun to be fired. The force of the ball striking the water near us had thrown us all violently into the sea. It had been a daring thing to do and one calling for very careful execution, for the slightest miscalculation might have killed us with the flying timbers of our boat.

"I give you your choice, Silver," I heard Dykes say. "If you come aboard, you are coming with your hands up and you are going to remain a prisoner in your cabin."

Silver now began to cajole and to make promises. He would waive his right to the one-fourth of the treasure. He would divide it, share and share alike, for every man on board no matter what his rank. He made an appeal to every man, asking if his proposition were not just.

"There's no argument about that," Dykes assured him. "You are done with the treasure already."

"But you can't mean to leave it behind," remonstrated Silver. "Think of sailing away from that much money when it's as good as between your decks." He was quick to see that he was making an impression on the crew, so he continued in that vein. "Think what it will mean to have all that gold where we could get our hands on it. We've got to stand together and get it aboard."

"Nothing to be gained on that tack, Lopez," replied Cowden.

"No," agreed Dykes. "Only one thing concerns you—are you coming aboard?"

Silver looked up and weighed his chances. Dykes had him covered and it would be foolish to attempt to fire upon him from the water. He bowed his head in bitter realization that his dream of magnificence had come to an end.

"I might have known it," he said almost with a sob. "As soon as MacGregor's ship appeared, I knew that ill-luck was after me, but I thought I could beat it."

"Coming aboard or not?" interrupted Dykes with cold impatient tone.

"I'm coming. What is there left to do? Where could I get in an open boat, even if you should let me try? I know when the game is up."

"Then be quick about it. And keep your hands high on the rope, or you'll drop back and sink out of sight."

"You won't have any trouble." Silver was obeying orders to the letter.

"No," said Dykes firmly, "we won't have any trouble."

It was a keen-eyed but very crestfallen Silver who came aboard. He was quickly relieved of all weapons and bound hand and foot until his cabin could be emptied of everything that might aid him to oppose us. Then we unbound him and locked him in. As he watched our procedure, he seemed suddenly to collapse. Hope had been taken from him, and the descent to dull certainties left him no support for his proud spirit.

CHAPTER XXI

Gold at Last

THE burden of our future action now devolved upon Dykes whose plan had been responsible for thwarting the sinister purposes of Lopez Silver. He was formally made captain, since such an officer fitted into the conventional way of handling a ship at sea. After a short conference with those under him, he was able to learn that they were unanimous in their desire to look further for Murray's treasure. He did not dare oppose them in this and so deferred to their wishes.

"Do you think it can be found?" he asked Dirk a little doubtfully.

Dirk smiled. "I think it will be no great task now."

The new captain, therefore, sent every able-bodied man ashore under Dirk's command to look for treasure. As soon as our party had landed, Dirk picked up a spade, walked down the path into the jungle a little way toward the old cache, and turned to face us.

"Dig from that tree this way," he directed. "Follow the path. They buried it in the path and walked over it to tramp the ground hard and smooth."

We could scarcely believe him, for to our eyes there was no sign that the earth had ever been disturbed. Nevertheless, we fell to, and found that after a little our picks and spades went into the soil easily. Almost at once there was a shout from one of the men which caused all of us to become much excited. And as our own spades struck upon the chests of coin and bundles of bar silver, we made the island ring with our shouts of delight.

It was almost dark when the last of the treasure went aboard and we clambered up after it. Dykes had had it all piled by the mast where every man could see it, and when the last chest was set in place, and all the men had come aboard, we crowded around to view our great wealth.

"Nine-hundred thousand pounds!" exclaimed one of the men. "Enough in my slice of it to make me richer than I ever dreamed I'd be! I can go home and take it easy for the rest of my days. No more sailing in my shirt before the mast. No more storms and battles and fevers and wounds. I can take it easy. So can ye all, bullies!"

"Not quite nine-hundred thousand pounds," Dykes hastened to say. "You remember that Silver divided one of the chests of doubloons among you on the very day it was found."

"Aye, that we do," said Cowden. "And where is all that gold now? Gone. Gambled away or cast overboard when we buried the men after we took *The Bristol*."

"Not with Silver on deck to see that all the men's effects went to his cabin to be disposed of as he saw fit," Dirk answered. "He took it from their pockets and out of their chests. And no one knows what he found on *The Bristol.*"

There was a growl of anger at this which threatened to demand that Silver divulge his loot and stand punishment.

"Let him keep his plunder," said Dirk with contempt. "I am not one to take the possessions of the dead."

There was an instant hush. The men were awed by Dirk's way of describing Silver's offense. They turned now to gloat over the pile of chests by the mast, as if this were cleaner gold, and to indulge long, long thoughts.

"Tell ye wot, Bub," said one of the sailors, breaking the silence. "I've been thinking I might have enough in my slice to be able to give some of it away. I have a sister that will never know need again if I git ashore safe. And if my father and mother are still alive, they are going to have a cottage, and a garden with flowers in it, and plenty of time to look at them. That is what I am going to do."

"And there's a girl I know—I might git married," blurted out another amid the laughter and banter of his mates. His face became crimson but he did not recede from his statement.

"Where shall we put all this tonight?" I asked.

"I move we leave it right where it is," Dirk replied. "Every man can see it here and know at once that we still have it."

A babble of approval greeted Dirk's words. "Three cheers for Monsma, bullies!" someone shouted, and they were given with a roar that could be heard far in the stillness of the evening.

After we had taken our evening meal and come back on deck, someone started a song and the ship rang with the rollicking songs which I had heard so many times before. But they were inclined to parody the lines to suit the whim, and roar their banter at one another in great glee. Then Silver's name was taken up and the men approached his cabin and sang lustily:

Butler took Silver's knife in the throat,
Yo-ho-ho, and a bottle of rum!
But all Silver got was a rusty groat,
Yo-ho-ho, and a bottle of rum!

Now Silver's hanging all dried and brown,
Yo-ho-ho, and a bottle of rum!
A-rattlin' his chains in New York Town,
Yo-ho-ho, and a bottle of rum!

There was much laughter and wicked jesting to follow, and Silver must have writhed under it and spent some time in pondering the strange mischances which overtake the rover and his ship.

It was to Dyke's credit and good judgment that very little rum flowed in the celebration. He ordered up a noggin for each man and reminded all hands that it was too early yet to think of abandoning ourselves to unrestricted celebration. As a matter of fact we had need now for even greater watchfulness and efficiency on the part of every man aboard. It was quite well known that *The Isabella* was a pirate craft and there were no doubt king's ships sailing the seas in search of her. We were too short-handed to meet with any untoward circumstances. Even the loss of one man from the line of duty might make all the difference between the destruction of the ship and making port safely.

"We are a long way from home," he said. "And outside of New York, where I am known and could enter port with few questions asked, there is no harbor that we dare approach. And we'll get to New York only by staying fit and by keeping a weather eye out for trouble. If it happens that we are compelled to run for it, we'll need all the skill and good luck this crew can possibly hope to muster."

He sobered them by his words, and they began to regard the treasure thoughtfully. "Aye, Captain," said Cowden, the self-constituted spokesman of the crew. "And it's well you told us. We were about to forget that we ain't through yet. And if we do get through, we got to keep sober and handle this craft shipshape. We thank you, and we'll do it."

THE pirates were sent to their quarters shortly after this and a watch was set over the treasure, but all hands talked, and the night wore on and the day came. Dirk was out of bed early and was busy getting ready to lift anchor and sail away. He had a British ensign which he had carried out of Silver's cabin, and he asked Dykes for permission to fly it aloft. He felt it would be best to show the colors of our nation as a way of giving the impression that our motives were honest.

"Our real difficulty is with the ship itself," Dykes said. "It is too well known to be easily disguised, and we'll no doubt be recognized by the first ship that sights us. It will be no easy job to bring her safe to port."

"If we take two days, and use every man, we could repaint," Dirk replied. "That might increase our chances."

"The very thing," Dykes exclaimed. "Get all hands at it. We'll take the time. Even months spent to guarantee safety is no loss of time when we have so much at stake."

Cowden was summoned to rig up some swings and to go overside with the men. "We plan to give her a new coat of paint," Dykes explained. "We thought it might increase our chances of getting through if we put a new suit on her."

"Aye, Captain, and it might—if it's the right color."

"The right color? What color ought she to be?"

"Well, something she hasn't been before, I'd say. She was gray when I first saw her, and she kept that color for two years. Then she was as black as night for a year and made a great reputation for being as black as she looked. We made her white before going north and had a few brushes to inform everybody that she had changed her skin. She ought not to be any of them colors, and yet, a change might be sure to give us away. You see she has a habit of changing, and they'll be expecting us to look different."

"That's not very assuring," Dykes replied with a serious face. "But I think we'll make the change just the same, if we can. Have you any paint aboard other than the colors you mentioned?"

"We laid in a lot of red paint when we got the white. We ain't used it. I was always thinking Silver would use it when he got ready to make port somewhere."

"Then we'll use it. If Silver felt the need to change her coat now and then, we'll be wise to follow his example. Get those slings overside. You ought to be able to use some of the wounded men for the job. And with every available man working briskly we ought to be under way in two or three days."

"Aye, aye, Captain," Cowden responded, turning to his task with energy.

The sea was calm for the next four days and we rode the soft swell to leeward of The Dead Man waiting for the task of repainting to be completed. The hull was made a vivid red and the masts and upper deck were gilded. When the job was done, Cowden rowed away some little distance to take a look at her. He returned by no means easy in his mind.

"I ain't so sure we've done the right thing," he declared. "We've made every line in her stand out. Mates, she takes your breath away! She looks a picture the way we've got her togged out. And she's powerful and swift as a bird! If I saw her chasing me, I'd never give up as long as I had a shot in my locker. I'd know she was a pirate craft. You don't need to be afraid of any other vessel in her trade. They'll just take one look and give us a wide berth, but I'd keep my distance from king's ships, you can lay to that."

This was disturbing news, but there was nothing for it now but to up anchor and sail as we were. To eliminate all risk was of course impossible, no matter what we did. Since it seemed improbable that we would be immediately recognized as *The Isabella*, we might be permitted to go our way unmolested. The idea of changing her name was not once thought of, for what a ship is called when she takes to the water she must remain if bad luck is not to follow her. Having done what we could do to disguise her, we made sail and laid course toward the north and east. By great good luck we might slip through and get home.

CHAPTER XXII

The End of Silver

As soon as the ship was under way, Lopez Silver appeared to be greatly excited. "Where are you?" he demanded when I brought him his breakfast on the first morning out. His eyes blazed and smouldered as he questioned me.

"How should I know?" I replied as indifferently as possible. "I am only the cabin-boy. The captain doesn't consult me when he comes to lay the course."

"Does that buckskin lubber who is steering her know?"

"He thinks so at any rate."

"And where does he think he is taking us?"

"New York, no doubt."

"No doubt!" Silver exclaimed sarcastically. "No doubt! Now I'll tell you where he is actually going—to Davy

Jones! And lucky he'll be to land us there instead of in Execution Dock!"

So genuine was Silver's apprehension that I spoke to Dirk about him. "He is really worried, I think. He scarcely tasted his food."

"Oh, there are any number of things to make him cross and excitable," Dirk answered. "For one thing—time is passing. Every day makes his chance of getting his hands on the treasure more unlikely. Perhaps he already knows he hasn't one chance in ten thousand. He will compose himself and eat his meals with appetite enough when he finally gives up all thought of regaining his ship. Give him time."

And that ended the matter for the next three days. Then, when it became apparent that Silver was truly worried about the fate of the vessel, I approached Dirk a second time. We decided to hear what Silver had to say and went to his cabin. When we made our business known he assumed the pose of an outraged lion. His head was up, his eyes were burning wells of indignation, and his general manner that of a man who had suffered unmentionable indignities at the hands of his inferiors.

"What do you think you are doing, Monsma?" he snapped.

"Sailing the ship, and keeping a good watch over you." Dirk met his glance steadily.

"Do you ever look at your charts?"

Dirk smiled provokingly. "Are the king's ships to be located on the charts?"

"Just the same, you'd better get your location and know where you are. And you'd better do it at once. You can't go blundering about in these waters. There's islands and shoals and reefs and king's ships and storms to think about. You've already had about all the luck that reasonable men could expect to have. So far you've had good weather, but you can't tell when it will change and give you all the work that a full crew could handle. And you haven't a full crew."

We assured him that we could not do other than take the risk. And though our decision irked him and made him splutter in towering wrath, we succeeded finally in making it clear to him that he must resign himself to whatever came. This he tried to do and seemed finally to grow more quiet as the days passed.

But he never ceased to ask about our course and whether or not we had sighted any vessels. In the end we permitted him to come out of his cabin and to satisfy himself as to the ship's position. But we kept him so completely at our mercy that he could not help knowing that nothing he could do would return him his ship and the treasure.

"How did you do it, Monsma?" he asked, after finding our location and noting the direction in which we were sailing. "If you hold on this course you will encounter practically no vessels sailing east or west. However, we are not safe from ships that may be looking for us. Keep a good lookout and let her drive."

Silver's relief was evident. What could be the reason? He must have known already from the sun and the movement of the ship that we were not far off the track. I saw that Dirk was also puzzled as we locked the door of the cabin and turned away.

"Perhaps we are not doing so well, after all," I ventured. "Any thing that makes Silver feel more comfortable disturbs me."

"I think he will not try to get us into trouble," said Dirk slowly. "There's no reason why he should want someone else to have the treasure. And he'll not likely send us into some nest of pirates that will butcher all hands. It is my opinion that he is anxious to get to land where he will have an outside chance of giving us the slip."

We held on the course for three days and on the morning of the fourth turned a point more to the north. We had sighted neither land nor ship so far. The sky was clear and the sea comparatively calm. Silver was in hopeful mood and we could hear him humming snatches of the songs of the sea as he paced the floor of his cabin. As for Monsma and the rest of us, we were not so happy. Anything that could cause Lopez Silver to break into song was under the circumstances almost sure to bode ill for us. And yet, we were unquestionably coming nearer home every hour.

On the sixth day we sighted land to the west and north of us. After going over our maps and charts, we could make nothing of it. There was really only one thing to do, to bring Silver on deck again and have him tell us where we were.

"It looks like the Carolinas to me," he stated. "And if your reckoning is as it should be, you are just outside Charles Town harbor. That is your chance to get a full crew, Monsma. You can sail in and pick enough men to take you on to New York. You've continued lucky, but I wouldn't invite trouble longer if I were you. You can't tell what will happen off this coast at this season of the year. I'd play as safe as possible."

We could not yet bring ourselves to believe that Silver did not have some ulterior motive in mind when he advised us, but since his counsel seemed the only safe course to pursue, we decided to abide by it. Accordingly, we slipped quietly into Charles Town bay after dark, rigged up a sling and dropped it overside, and helped Dykes to get a firm footing upon it. He was busy there for some time with a bucket of paint and a brush, laboring by the light of the rising moon. Then he came on deck to announce that our ship was *The New York* and that *The Isabella* was no more.

"I'll go ashore tomorrow and look for hands to take us the rest of the way," he confided. "It will be well for us to rid ourselves of bad company as early as possible."

The next morning the men were told that they might have their release at once if they so desired. There was almost a shout of delight at this news. Ships could be found here bound for many different ports. That would permit the men to put the past behind them and out of mind. And each man had every reason to wish to make good his escape with his share of the treasure. All hands were summoned to the mast, and the division was justly apportioned according to agreement. It was a happy crew that rowed away with Dykes. They waved to us farewells and expressed, no doubt, genuine and heartfelt words of good will.

We had no trouble in getting men for the ship. A storm had driven two vessels ashore, and a considerable number of their crews had been rescued. They were sailors from New England ports and quite anxious to make their way home. We took them on, with instructions to come aboard that evening.

We conferred then with Silver. He talked with us guardedly until he learned that it was our intention to set him ashore. Then he smiled in evident pleasure and became much more spontaneous in what he said.

"After all, it's much better than a trip to England in chains," he declared. "I certainly had everything planned to end the voyage differently, but to miss Execution Dock after the streak of ill luck I've had is not to end in complete disaster. This is a quiet place on the whole, and I can remain here without exciting too many questions until I can find something to do. This time I'll try to get a place where there's little danger of someone shivering my timbers."

His eyes darted to each of our faces as if he would wring from us some clue to the drift of our thoughts.

"I'll tell you this much, Silver," volunteered Dykes. "You've had your timbers shivered this trip as you say. At any rate you've lost your part of Murray's cache, but we do not care to rob you of your ship into the bargain. We'll send *The New York* back to you in ballast to Charles Town as soon as we have opportunity. What you do with her after that is none of our business, but if you are wise, you'll sell her, or put her in other hands in honest trade. As for the trouble you have cost us first and last, we shall try to forget it."

"That's decent of you, Dykes," Silver answered. Then with a twinkle in his eyes, "She is a good ship, is *The New York*. I should realize a nice sum for her if I sell. As for taking her to sea myself—that is all over. I'll get my money out of her and slip away to join my family. You didn't know I was married I suppose, but I am. And now that I shall be done with the sea, I'll buy a plantation and settle down to a quiet life. Treasure hunting has its reverses like everything else."

"You might try The Dead Man once more," suggested Dirk. "You might come on something there eventually."

SILVER stared at him with astonished eyes. "What—what do you mean?"

"Simply that there's a great deal of treasure still there," said Dirk. "That day you sent me into the growth to look around I saw something that had been put there many years ago. There were chests by the dozen sticking out of the earth. The wood had rotted, and the chests were yawning out doubloons in a great golden stream. There must have been at least twice as much as was contained in this cache."

Lopez Silver was not the only one to show surprise. We were all at him to tell us more.

"Why didn't you tell us while we were there?" asked Dykes, recovering somewhat from his daze.

"I thought we had enough to do to get off safely with what we had. Anyway, it was not the treasure we were trying to find. I thought it would be something for Silver to hunt a second time, and besides I didn't want you and Darby to be dragged off with him when he went."

Lopez Silver's eyes danced in spite of every effort to mask his emotions. "Ordinarily I'd not believe you, Monsma. But I happen to know that Andrew Murray made many a rich haul during his career and that no living man knew where he did his banking. My father tried often to interest Flint in sticking to Murray's heels and tracing it, but Flint was not a man who could plan and wait for anything. If he had been given his choice of a hundred thousand pounds at once or ten millions if he waited, he would have taken the one hundred thousand every time. So that is where Murray stowed it away, is it? Any one should have known it from his having put his slice of the loot from *The Santissima Trinidad* there."

He considered a moment, looked at his hands, glanced out at the bay, and back to us. "A week ago I would have jumped at it, Monsma," he went on. "But that is over now. I've been through a great many dangers, even at my age. Taking things by and large, I've been more than lucky. I have come through safe and sound and with enough to live comfortably. I think I shall not tempt fate and Father Neptune any further. However, you might tell me something more about this fabulous pile of gold you saw, Monsma. It will make a good story to tell over a noggin of rum when I am old and begin to recall old times."

Dirk laughed softly. "So it would! But you don't need to know exactly the amount or just where it is located. Such stories never are exact, not even when a map is furnished."

Silver joined in the laugh at his expense, although his eyes betrayed his disappointment. His tongue, however was ready enough.

"I think I'll tell them it is on the west side of the island and a little to the left of that nose of rock at the south-west corner. It's that rock that is the clue. And I'll need to give them something to make it seem true."

"Not so bad at guessing after all, are you?" replied Monsma. "Well, I give it to you. But I'll not help you find it, and you need not come north begging me to go along either."

The conference broke up in good humor, and Silver arose to take his leave of the ship. Four men were called in to carry his chests to the rail and to lower them into a boat. I went down with him to help him ashore and to bring the boat back. He was very careful of his two large chests, and, judging from the way the four men tugged at them, they were well filled.

"You'll see *The New York* in about a month, I should judge," Dykes assured him as he took his leave. "And better luck next time."

"And a big slice of the other treasure," said Monsma.

"I won't look for it for some time, you can be sure of that much," Silver answered. "One way and another, I've managed to lay something by. It's safe ashore and ready to be used whenever I want it. And first and last, this voyage is not altogether a failure. Those chests have a little real money in them—enough at any rate that I'll not land entirely empty-handed."

I brought the boat in to the wharf and together, after a struggle requiring all our strength and skill, the chests were landed. Silver stood beside them and smiled down upon me as I took my seat once more in the boat.

"Well, Darby McGraw," he addressed me in good-natured banter, "a fair wind and a safe voyage when you put out for treasure hereafter. I shall expect to hear that you have become master of your own ship some day."

I protested that I was through with the sea and that nothing could possibly entice me away from land again.

"She has a pull, Darby, does the sea. She is a mistress you can't always deny. I have known a great many men who went home declaring that they were done with her forever. But she drew them back, and in the end she took them all."

He turned as he finished speaking and

his eyes rested upon an unusually handsome negress who stood inconspicuously near a pile of casks and boxes.

"Here, girl," Lopez called to her. "Help a poor sailor get his tricks safe somewhere."

She came toward him obediently, her soft eyes regarding him quietly, and, I thought, proudly. She lifted the largest chest as if it had been a child and set it easily upon her head. Then she tucked the other one under her arm and, with a smile of inexpressible adoration at Silver, moved off up the dusty street. Silver with a final wave of the hand in my direction turned to follow her.

I sat in the boat and watched them until they were far up the street, where, from a deep doorway a man emerged to join them. The three stood in the shadow of a building and I could not see them very distinctly from where I sat, but I had a pronounced feeling that the man who had joined Lopez and the negress was an aged sailor who walked with a crutch. Still in the shadow, they turned a corner of the building and passed out of sight, but not until the bobbing form of the older man had confirmed my first impression of him.

I had no longer any doubt that the story of Long John's death had been circulated by that wily old fox himself so that he might close his days undisturbed. And I knew why Lopez Silver had fumed and fretted in his cabin and had given us no peace of mind until he had learned that our course would bring us directly to Charles Town. It was there that his father awaited him. He had found him, and had brought home enough plunder to last for many days. Perhaps he might be satisfied with what he had and have no more to do with the sea.

CHAPTER XXIII

The Victors

OUR crew came aboard toward evening and a single glance was sufficient to show us that we had secured some of the best men that ever went to sea. They were strong, alert, in good health, and as hard and weather-beaten as the rocks along their coast. They knew their business and took up their tasks cheerfully. It was naturally somewhat disturbing to us to mark their surprise when they saw the number of guns we carried, but we had a story ready for them. Our vessel had been a pirate ship. She had been captured and sold to us as a prize. We were taking her home and had simply engaged a crew to man her until we could reach Charles Town. We had, therefore, engaged the present crew to bring us on to New York.

There may have been some doubt of the truth of our story, but true or not it could not be disproved. And since we did not have the look of pirates, we were taken for honest men and the ship was soon at sea.

The voyage was uneventful. We arrived in New York harbor on time and cast anchor in the early morning six days out of Charles Town. Our men were eager to go ashore and to try to get a berth on some one of the numerous vessels then in port. Each man was paid generously and took his departure with gruff but kindly expressions of good wishes for Captain Dykes, for the mate Dirk Monsma, and for Darby McGraw, the cabin-boy. The ship was presently deserted, leaving the three officers at liberty to discuss plans for getting the treasure ashore and to devise some story to explain why we had returned by sea.

After a somewhat lengthy debate, we decided to remain where we were until after nightfall, then in the darkness we would bring the treasure off in one of the boats and conceal it in the warehouse of our company. If the plan went well we would be able to stow it away without being seen; and though suspicion might be aroused later, there would be nothing on board to betray us. We, therefore, kept to the captain's cabin for the most part and talked or dozed comfortably in the luxurious chairs until the sun had finally disappeared in the west. Then we broke out our treasure so that we might send it overside as soon as darkness had come.

"So far all goes well," said Dykes as he looked at the immense amount of wealth stacked before him. "In two hours we ought to have it ashore and safe for the present. It scarcely seems possible after all it has cost in toil and blood that we are to get it almost without effort. But believe it or not, that is how it will be."

And so it was. We made each trip back and forth so skillfully that we were not nailed once in the darkness. To be sure, our labor was greatly facilitated by the watchman at the warehouse who immediately recognized us and helped us stow everything away. By eleven o'clock we were back aboard our ship and ready to retire.

"Tomorrow," said Dykes as he bade us good-night, "we'll go ashore openly and explain the manner of our coming. I think we'll have no trouble on that score. Now that the treasure is out of the ship we can feel more or less secure, no matter what suspicions may be aroused. And if we send the vessel back to Charles Town within a day or two, the matter will be quickly forgotten."

THE rest is briefly told. We were welcomed by Ormerod and Corlaer with open arms and had no difficulty with the authorities. Any irregularity was easily overlooked, for our company had great influence in the town because of its history for honesty and square-dealing. The story that we had been entrusted with the responsibility of bringing the ship to port and of sending it on to Charles Town seemed plausible enough since we often acted as agents in the coastwise trade. And when *The New York* departed the third day following, in command of a dependable captain and an honest crew, our anxiety ended, and we had our first moment of untroubled repose since our capture on the St. Lawrence river so many months before.

Naturally the fur company of Ormerod and Corlaer began to branch out in its activities until it became known as the richest and most powerful company in North America. But it was not until after a considerable time had elapsed that Dykes, Monsma and I consented to take any position of prominence with it. By that time there were few to remember that we had once entered port on board a vessel that bristled with heavy guns.

THE END

"AW, LET THE KID HIT"

By Michael Avallone

When you feel like going soft on a rookie batsman—even with an eleven-run spread in your favor—better figure first how to explain it to your dutiful, hot-blooded catcher.

THE HAWKS had piled up so many runs at the expense of the Browns that even the most rabid of baseball fans were beginning to yawn when the seventh inning rolled around.

Substitutes were rolling out of the loudspeaker like water.

"Oll batting for Cassidy!"

The crowd could be forgiven this once for not sitting up and taking notice. Hawk hitters had nailed the lid down with a staggering total of sixteen safeties and were walking away from a 12-1 score.

Roxy Carter's educated fast ball had left the guys who batted for the Brown cause speechless. It looked like a red letter day for the Hawk nine all around.

"Oll batting for Cassidy!"

No one noticed the change in the lineup. Not a ripple of response, approval or otherwise, came down from the seats. The Browns had blown the game and had let the Hawks, a cocky first place outfit, climb all over them. Partisan Brownie fans were disgusted.

12-1. How much of a rooter can you be?

Out on the mound, Roxy Carter hitched his pants and waited for the pinch hitter to step in. Oll. A rookie fresh up from Peoria. So what? Three swings at big league pitching and he'd be on the bus heading back. Crazy game this, thought Roxy.

Roxy Carter was big league pitching, too.

Eighteen wins, six of them shutouts and this was only the beginning of August. He was having one of his biggest years. His sidearm curve was pushing the Hawks right to the flag.

As he glanced down the line to his battery mate, Deacon Doyle, he grinned broadly. The new guy standing up there facing him in the batter's box was holding a bat so big it made a lumber yard of home plate. Rookies always interested him, always gave him a chance to work a few things.

This was just another wide-shouldered kid trying to crash the big time. Well, let's see what he's got to sell.

Roxy had an eleven run cushion and only two innings more to work. The Browns were acting like doormats and he was in a stepping mood. They'd been popping his stuff up all afternoon and only nicked him for three singles. The first two batters in the seventh had broken their backs on his soft tantalizing curve. Two outs.

Why should this kid Oll be any different?

Pitcher-like, he took the kid in. Sixty feet separated them but Roxy's practiced eye narrowed it down to talking distance.

Hmmm. Big, strong looking.

Shoulders are plenty broad. Doesn't look scared either. The way most bushers look in their first at bat in the big time. Never heard of this guy before. Must be a new one.

Well, let's try him first. Then we'll know if he's just another green pea.

NOTHING like a good fast ball across the letters to find out what kind of a batter you're tangling with. Roxy reared back on his right leg and let fly. The ball split the afternoon air like a comet. Deacon Boyle gloved it and the guy in blue behind him roared, "Stee—rike one!"

He rested on his hip and took the return throw.

What's-his-name, Oll, hadn't budged an inch. The pitch had cut the plate in half but he hadn't fallen away from it. The kid's either stupid or has guts. Maybe

Roxy shook off Boyle's signal—tossed a sizzling fast ball that was all steam and no curve.

both. Haven't found out which. Anyway, nothing lost. One up on him now. He'll be waiting for a good one, so——

Roxy's soft curve butterflyed around the edges of the plate for a one-and-one count. It was close but not quite in there. A perfect sucker pitch.

Kid's got an eye, he thought. Most bushers would have tried to murder that one.

Noises of impatience went around the stands. Roxy Carter didn't notice.

Oll, he watched now with respect. His pitcher's eye had him marked. He had decided the big kid was a good hitter even though he hadn't seen him swing once. Only a really good pitcher can do that.

He chuckled suddenly. Why not? The score was 12-1. Two out. Nobody on. How much could he hurt himself?

Even if the kid did connect—hell, it would be worth it just to see if he was right. He shook off Deacon Boyle's signal and came in again with a sizzling fast ball that was all steam and no curve. Just a high, hard one made to order for power hitters.

As a prophet, Roxy batted .1000.

Oll, who had given a good imitation of still life up until then, kicked into action like a supercharger. His arms, legs and bat did a chain reaction routine and Roxy Carter's fastest delivery tore a seat apart in the upper left field deck.

The crowd watched in stunned disbelief as the big, broad-shouldered rookie lumbered around the bases for a homer. Disbelief turned into a bedlam of wild cheers.

Roxy was delighted. He'd been right, of course. Should have known by the way the kid held that right shoulder of his in the dropped position at the beginning of his swing. Batters get real power that way. Roxy knew. Hadn't he pitched against the best of them in his time?

Oll was practically mobbed by his teammates around home plate. The game was past rescue, of course, but a homer off the likes of Roxy Carter was something. First time up in the majors and he gets a homer. How about that?

Roxy set his chin and blazed through the rest of the game with ease. No Brown batter got on after Oll. The all-or-nothing-all technique gave him another big one for the win column and pushed the Hawks a full six games ahead of the runner-up Cubs.

Lacing his street shoes in the locker room, Roxy looked up to see Deacon Doyle towering over him. The big catcher still had his dirty uniform on. A look of resentment was pinching his heavy face.

"How come you shake off my sign on that kid in the seventh? I signalled for a curve." Boyle fairly ripped it out.

Roxy grinned. "Wanted to see what he could do with it."

Boyle's face kept its pinched look. "Well, you saw. He hit it a mile. What's the matter with you, Roxy?" He bit the words off like they were chaws of tobacco.

THE PITCHER dropped his hands to his sides. It was the old story again. Who's more important? The catcher or the pitcher?

"I don't get you, Deac."

"Listen, Roxy, I'll make it plain." Boyle moved in belligerently. "I don't know what satisfaction you get outa lettin' rookies tag you for homers and I don't care. All I do care about is this. I'm callin' them behind the plate. Me. Got that?"

The pitcher straightened and got to his feet. Roxy's locker was in the corner of the clubhouse and they were alone except for a couple of ball players down at the far end of the room.

Roxy's jaw set in a hard line and his eyes lost the warm, friendly look usually found in them.

"You're a little mixed up, aren't you, boy?" His voice was cucumber cool which only seemed to make Boyle's voice get louder.

"Yeah? If it wasn't for my signals, me doling out the right signals, mixin' them up for you, that soup bone of yours would have folded months ago. I know how to save your wing. You don't."

"You'd better shut up, Deac." Roxy's voice was even lower now. He was sore. Plenty sore. Boyle had sounded off on the same subject too many times. Why, the bum would be down on some hot, Texas team now if he, Roxy, hadn't asked Manager Wilks to give him a break. Gratitude!

Boyle ignored him. "Listen, Carter. The catcher runs the battery, not the pitcher. Cut the tricks. I'll decide what you throw and what you don't throw. Next time you shake a sign off when it's called, I'll ram the ball down your throat!"

They were close to each other now, angry words flying fast when some spittle from Boyle's mouth flew between his teeth and landed squarely on Roxy's face.

That did it. What had been just a disagreement over tactics now became something else.

Roxy balled up a fist and rammed it into the catcher's left eye. Boyle howled in pain. The pitcher, lighter of the two, rushed him and flailed with his arms. It was a game, but futile, gesture. Boyle stood his ground and protected his head with his arms. The blows staggered him but Roxy didn't have enough weight to back them up. The heavier catcher reached out, blocked his swings and threw a punch of his own.

Crack!

His meaty fist sent Roxy crashing into a locker door that opened into the aisle and the game hurler went down. Swearing violently, Boyle went after him, throwing one punch after the other. The room began to dance before Roxy's eyes.

Stunned by the unexpectedness of the fight and cowed by Deacon Boyle's rep as a back alley fighter, the other players held back. Roxy Carter was taking his lumps unassisted. The insensate Boyle might have wrecked the pennant chances of the Hawks beyond repair if the big green kid hadn't suddenly loomed in the doorway.

One big hand plucked Boyle backwards and spun him around.

The catcher's mouth showed his astonishment. He recognized Oll in the split second before the kid's huge right hand rocked him off his feet. A left hook, even harder than the right, sent him crashing to the floor.

He was flat on his back, out. The dazed Roxy was helped to his feet by suddenly remorseful teammates. He sat down heavily on a bench and struggled to open his eyes. He got them wide open and grinned.

Deacon Boyle was a silent heap on the floor.

ROXY looked around some more and spotted the big, wide-shouldered kid standing by, looking bashful about something.

"Say——" he began and groaned. Blood was running from his split lips. Oll held out a handkerchief in his thick fingers and Roxy took it.

"Don't talk, Mr. Carter. You're bleeding bad."

Roxy nodded and winced. He shook his head. "The Deacon really gets some cute ideas. Thanks, kid."

The rookie smiled down at him proudly and said, "Shucks. It was a pleasure, Mr. Carter."

"Good thing you happened by, that's all. He would have killed me."

Suddenly, as if sensing a bond between them, Oll dropped on the bench beside him. "What happened? I always thought catchers and pitchers were pals."

"Don't you believe it!" Roxy shot it out, dabbing at his mouth with the handkerchief. "Take me and Boyle there. We get along like married people—Hey!—it's all your fault, too!"

Oll looked hurt.

"I don't see what you mean, Mr. Carter."

Roxy was not to be turned.

"Back there in the seventh—and don't call me Mister Carter—I gave you a high, hard one when Deac signalled for a curve. You got four bases on it and he got ulcers. He gets mad as a wet hen when I shake off his sign. He's funny that way."

"I really got hold of that one, didn't I?" the Kid wasn't bragging, he simply said it.

Roxy stopped wiping his mouth in bewilderment. "Say, what the hell are you doing in here anyway? I've been in baseball ten years and never saw an opponent in the rival locker room yet."

Oll's big, pleasant face dropped like one of Roxy's own deliveries. He compressed his lips so that his nostrils flared. A deep, red flush made his face comical.

"Well—I—you see——"

"Out with it. You spying on us for the Browns or something?"

"Oh, no, no!" The kid was vehement in his protests. "Nothing like that. It's just that this was my first game of major league ball——"

"Go on."

"Well, I got a homer today in my first at bat, pinch hitting besides and I sorta wondered——"

Roxy looked at the red handkerchief in his hands. "I suppose I owe you a favor. If you hadn't come by when you did——"

"Well," Oll rushed it out, "I was wondering, seeing as how you're my first homer victim, could I have your autograph, Mr. Carter?"

THE SEVENTH BULLET

By Murray Leinster

THE first thing that Pedro saw after being born, squealing, was a gin bottle. By that you gather that his mother was a remarkable sort of woman. As a matter of fact, she was. She usually passed as a Kanaka—and this was in Cambodia—but there was some Chinese, and more than a little Malay, and probably a few drops of Negrito, Siamese, and God knows what other blood in her veins. Pedro never remembered her very well, as she was stabbed by another woman when he was five, and never had the opportunity to ask her who his father was. In any event, there is some doubt as to whether she could have told him.

Pedro was left to the tender mercies of the world at her death, and fared badly until he was taken in hand by an old Chinaman as a work of benevolence. He knifed the Chinaman, later, in the ruined, royal palace of the deserted city of Angkor-Thom, lying hidden up the Tunle-Sap, for an entirely mythical belt of gold-pieces. He then fared forth over the world upon his own.

He was not so badly equipped, considering everything. He was an experienced man of the world, with all the accumulated vices of all the mongrel races in his veins. His head was a marvel to look at, and got him the post of body-servant to a worthy German anthropologist who studied him as the most interesting of his specimens. Then, too, he knew a trick or so of knife-play, had a coward's regard for his own skin, and knew all the entirely dubious tricks of the dark and devious Oriental. He was even educated, after a fashion. He had but a single weak point—he was religious.

Lest that seem a redeeming trait in his character, it had best be explained that it was a religion of his own contriving. It embraced magic, witchcraft, divination, thuggee, and real demonology. It had some few notions selected from Mohammedan theology and even a pat idea or so learned when he flirted momentarily with the Christian God. He had likewise a selection of superstitions learned from the German professor—the Black Mountain superstition of the Seventh Bullet in particular.

In that connection, which requires a compact with Satan, he had a perfectly clear and rather horrible idea of how to open communication with devils. All of his religion, however, was based upon practicality. Each of his beliefs was designed to add something to his own comfort or safety, and it was that habit of thought that indirectly led to the death of the Raja Kangsar of Raman.

The German professor was dead—his case had been diagnosed as fever of the arsenic variety—and Pedro had fled with a hundred pounds in gold. He squirmed across Cochin China and crossed the China Sea on a Burmese craft, and wound up in Yala, where the Raja caused his apprehension, fined him one hundred pounds in gold for entering his dominions, ordered him beaten on general principles, and forgot him.

But Pedro did not forget. With all the undesirable traits of a dozen races concentrated in his body, he could not forget. He was as venomous as a taunted cobra; wild to strike. He bathed the wounds of his beating and stewed in the juices of his own hate.

He was quite ripe for those who came to him. They were nobles of the tiny independent state, and they desired the Raja out of the way. It was essential that they should not appear in the matter, but they would pay very well for a suitable and thoroughly well-done murder.

Pedro knew why they came disguised. He knew why they refused their names. He knew that any attempt to disover who they were would result in his own immediate death.

The Malays have a number of very efficient third degrees. There is a little trick they have by which a palm-shoot is introduced into a man's body and grows up into his very vitals until he dies. It takes about four days for him to die, and long before that time he has told all he knows and all that he ever guessed, and is willing to sell his soul for a merciful bullet.

Surely, Pedro knew why they would not say who they were. It would be inconvenient for them if he should fail and be caught alive.

He accepted the commission, principally because of the help they would give him. He desired the death of the Raja himself. With their aid, and a little trick he knew of, the thing could be done very handily. Without his own special knowledge—particularly of the way to open communication with devils—it was very nearly hopeless.

The Raja was aware that he was not precisely popular. The larger part of his time was spent in a curious room that was set with mirrors, and it was an impossible thing to kill him in that room. The walls were mirrors, and they projected and shifted and moved about here and there, so that no man in that room ever knew whether he was looking at the Raja or at a reflection of that potentate in a mirror. It was a crystal maze, set up in Malasia, and no man could say that the Raja was within five feet of him or within five yards, nor in what direction. Any man in that room saw two dozen Rajas who moved in unison, and it was hopeless to shoot at random. One would merely shatter a mirror and spent the next four days—or five, if one were very strong—in a hell that would make Hades a paradise in comparison.

Still, Pedro accepted the task of

murdering the Raja, for five hundred pounds in gold. He went off into the forests to make his preparations. It would not be very pleasant to narrate them, and it would surely be very horrible It included doing things with a cat and a goat and a number of other unpleasant matters, and it would not sound very credible. It satisfied Pedro, however, and he returned with the firm conviction that he had made the compact of the Seventh Bullet, and that seven revolver cartridges he brought back were authentically enchanted.

That, in itself, does not seem very probable, but you must remember his upbringing. After a suitable sacrifice to King Tze, the God of Benevolent Fortune, he had once won forty-two pounds in a Chinese gambling house.

After strangling an apparently poverty-stricken Malay in the fashion chosen by devotees of Kali—Pedro had done it more as an experiment than anything else—he had found six sovereigns in the Malay's sash.

There were other of those sequences, so it was in no wise illogical from his point of view that he made a compact which charmed the seven bullets he put into an automatic pistol. Six of those bullets would go where Pedro desired them, infallibly hitting their mark, and the seventh could be directed by the devil. It was not an unfair deal. Surely, six sure shots in exchange for a single demoniac pellet of lead was not a bad bargain. One could kill six men with those six bullets, and at five hundred pounds apiece. . . .

He made his plans carefully, always counting upon the intervention of the devil as a perfectly practical aid, and making each of his other arrangements with the same severe practicality.

There was a man waiting with a boat for him. The man was bringing a certain sum in gold for the purchase of some entirely fictitious loot Pedro had promised to sell him. It was Pedro's notion that after the man had served his purpose, a knife would secure the gold he was bringing and would furthermore add a little to Pedro's store. Pedro was inherently an opportunist. What more natural than to arrange that his boatman should not only serve his convenience, but add a little to his wealth?

There was also a house into which Pedro purposed to slip if the chase were hot after him. He had bribed one of the servants and a way for his entry and exit was prepared. Pursuers would spend a long time searching for him there—and Pedro had a shrewd suspicion that something might be picked up if he were fortunate enough to reach the haven without anyone on his trail.

He arranged that the gold with which he was to be paid for the murder, was to be waiting for him. He would see it before firing the shot that finished the Raja, and would return for it. At the same time, he knew that it was the purpose of his employers to finish his career when he had ended that of the Raja. That was no more than a reasonable precaution on their part, lest he talk too freely afterward. But he had an idea of his own as to the outcome.

The matter came to a head upon a certain day when the houses of Yala were shimmering in the heat, when the forests were green and cool, when the women who went down to the little river to wash clothes had gone back into their homes until the heat of midday was past.

Over the streets and smells of Yala a drowsy, brooding silence rested. Only an occasional dog scratched himself in the mud, or a rooster crowed listlessly, or a naked brown baby played solemnly with a shapeless, unrecognizable toy.

In the royal palace the Raja sat drowsily in the room of the mirrors, nodding gently. The place was filled with the harmonious buzzing of flies, and had a scent compounded of rank perfumes and red plush carpet that covered the floor. Beside the Raja, a weak-faced eunuch squatted with a fan, with which he cooled the fat, gross face of royalty. There were only tiny, furtive rustlings in all the passageways of the palace, where barefooted folk moved silently, or slept.

Then, quite suddenly, Pedro slipped into the place of mirrors and was reflected in two dozen glasses. He raised an automatic pistol, and it was as if half a company of men had done the same. He fired—it seemed at one of the twenty-odd reflections of the Raja that were around him on every side. But no silvered pane cracked across. No *one* of the rotund reflections shattered into bits, yet the rest made curious gestures of terror and dismay in automatic, faithful imitation of the real Raja which might be any of their number. Pedro saw two dozen men fall coughing to the floor, while two dozen screaming eunuchs fled with identical, monkeylike movements through two dozen hidden doors.

The first of the seven bullets had found its mark.

Pedro had fled from the palace before the servants of the Raja rushed into the room of the mirrors, blundering against the glass walls that confused them. They ran helplessly against the walls, and cried out, wailing, because they saw their ruler lying bleeding upon the floor before them and could not find their way to his side. When finally one of their number had by sheer fortune reached the Raja's feebly moving form, it happened that he was a man whose son had cast covetous eyes upon a damsel the Raja had once desired. The matter was long since forgotten by most folk, but—if there had been any life left in the fat body when that man leaned over it, there was none when he turned to the others.

By this time Pedro had reached the man who held the bag of gold that was to reward him. He snatched at the gold—and barely missed the man's knife, as it cut upward for his belly. . . . He picked up the bag of clinking coins and fled before the man had ceased to writhe.

The second of the seven bullets had been fired.

The town was becoming a buzzing, milling hive of angry bees, alarmed and ready to strike at anyone or anything from sheer unrest, when Pedro found his way out of the palace gate. A huge man with a green turban barred his path, demanding news of what caused the disturbance in the palace. It was a public street, and the man wore a green turban—sure sign that he was descended from the Prophet. Pedro was in haste, and yet deplorably handicapped. He could not tarry, and he was more than a little frightened. He wrenched himself free and fled.

Then he heard the man's voice crying out. Pedro did not turn. He was suddenly smitten with terror. Without looking back, he flung the muzzle of his automatic behind him and fired at random. His bullets were enchanted, in any event. . . . He heard the man scream.

The third of the seven bullets had been fired.

He was calmer when he reached the boatman. In one of the houses of the city there was a cast-off costume which the assassin of the Raja had worn. Also there was a woman with a knife-wound in her throat, and her wristlets and anklets and the very bangles in her ears torn off, but Pedro's bag was a little heavier.

He went down the stream for two days, but the boatman stopped on a mud-bank a little below the city of Yala, with an expression of astonishment upon his face. Pedro gave the boatman no further thought. He had served his purpose, had added to Pedro's convenience and his wealth, and could safely be totally ignored.

On the third day he saw a barrier of logs across the stream, and strange, little, apelike soldiers on guard. They saw him, too, and fired at him. And then Pedro knew that they were hot upon his trail.

As a matter of fact, you see, Raman is a little kingdom over which Siam exercises a certain paternal care. The Raja may—and does—bleed and murder, hang and flay, not to mention other less pleasant methods of extinction, but after all, the Siamese look after the affairs of the kingdom. In turn the Siamese are looked after by a number of nations, each of whom would like very much to kick all the others out and do the looking after all by itself.

The net result of the complicated paternalism is that Siam and all its protected states are linked together by a complete system of telegraphy, and Pedro had not been half a day out of Yala before the word had gone silently before him along a slender wire. He had been described—and he was readily recognizable. One little feature of his countenance was past disguise. He had looked at an English woman, once, in Calcutta, and her escort had seen his expression. The result was an instinctive gesture on the Englishman's part which left Pedro with a broken nose, and left the Englishman with a sensation of uncleanliness until he had removed his glove and dropped it unobtrusively in the gutter. Broken noses are not common in Oriental countries, where men fight with knives and never with fists, and that one thing marked Pedro out at sight.

He knew that he was being sought for, and that they were aware that the man in the boat was their quarry. Being a wise man, he hit for the woods, leaving his boat by the side of the stream, but carrying the bag of gold and the anklets, and the few coins he had acquired from his boatman. He had, too, four bullets in his automatic, very marvelous bullets, because three of them would infallibly go wherever he wished them to go, though the fourth must go where the devil aimed.

It was a wise move, of course, to leave the stream, because they would have got him in another three minutes, magic bullets or no magic bullets.

In the jungle he was not especially safe. Your Malay is no woodsman. He is rarely to be found far from a stream.

Still, there are other races in Malasia with no such aquatic habits. There are the Semang, for instance, brown people with woolly hair and no clothes to speak of, who are commonly believed to be able to trail by scent like a dog. And the Sakai are no mean trackers, either. But give a Semang a bent leaf and a single footprint, not too old, and he will puff away into the jungle like a hound on a warm trail. It takes a clever man to puzzle a Semang. Doubling and redoubling may cause him to squat on his haunches a while and chew at a bit of betel, scratching his scaly hide the while—all of them have skin disease—but sooner or later he will puzzle out the track and be off again. And they put two Semang on Pedro's trail.

He was running desperately through the thick, humid undergrowth, the monster ferns and colossal lichens and mosses, tripping over the llianas and the creeping vines, a queer little man with a queerly-shaped head, his breath coming in gasps, a bag slung at his waist and an automatic in his sash. And as he ran his brain was racing madly for some trick that would get him out of his fix. The men who had hired him in the first place could not possibly be of help, now. He did not know their names, for one thing, and again he had slain one of their number. With a sudden clarity he realized that he could tell nothing that would hurt them. They would have no reason to interfere should he be tortured to make him tell what he knew. He knew nothing!

Sweat drenched him long before his exertion should have caused it. He was remembering a man he had once seen, a man three days gone in the torture of the bamboo shoot. The thing was growing slowly, inexorably into his vitals, its softly curled leaves thrusting aside muscle and tissue, tearing nerves and rending even bones. The man was fastened firmly to the ground, where that slender growing thing would eat into his body. He was rocking slowly back and forth, screaming voicelessly, no more than a racked whisper issuing from his lips. He was babbling, raving, utterly out of his mind, unable to think, to reason, to be aware of anything but the unspeakable agony that had taken him as a strong man and made him into a thing that could only suffer. And he had been in that state for three days and would live yet another day. There is a tradition, by the way, that no man who took this dire vengeance on an enemy by the torture of the bamboo shoot was ever left unsatisfied.

But not less than four days of such torment as he had once seen was waiting for Pedro if he were caught. He would be told to name those who had hired him—and he could not tell. He would be offered a bullet, he would be offered death as the ultimate of reward for a full confession, and long before the ending he would embrace the offer of death as the supreme of desirable things. But they would not give him the bullet. He would tell anyway, in a vain hope of placating them to murder, and the assassins of Rajas are made examples of, always....

His preoccupation with what waited for him made him leave a clear trail. The Semang followed it at a run with the Siamese soldiers close behind them. They would capture him and turn him over to the Raja's successor as a neighborly act, and Pedro would grow hoarse with screaming and rock back and forth, babbling, mad, and blind with utter agony.

He uttered his first cry of dismay when he plunged through a thick mass of undergrowth and saw water before him, and worse than merely water, saw a steam-launch with more soldiers standing upon it. He plunged to his left, his heart constricting a little. The vines and bushes whipped his face. His mongrel soul shivered. He could barely breathe. His eyes were wide and staring, but they saw nothing but the phantom of himself, bound down upon the ground and screaming terribly while a bamboo shoot bored slowly, patiently into and through his body. Beneath his swarthy skin he was gray with terror.

Then he heard a shrill yelp behind him and turned. Before he knew what he had done, he had wasted two of his precious remaining magic bullets upon a Semang and Siamese soldier.

Then he shrieked, for he realized what he had done. He had had seven bullets. Six of them would infallibly go where he desired them to go, but the seventh must go where the devil wished, *and his only remaining bullet was the Seventh Bullet!*

He saw himself surrounded by little monkeylike soldiers who advanced. He saw that they had ropes to bind him with. He knew what his fate would be if they caught him alive, and there was no possible way to make one bullet secure his escape, and even less chance to fight his way out with his knife. He had to be quick. And he was a coward.

He was wrenched and torn by the terrific conflict within him, his coward's fear of death, and his even more terrible fear of the fate that he knew awaited him. But it was not until one of the little brown men actually reached for him that he could break the spell of paralysis that rested upon him.

Pedro screamed, an unearthly, despairing scream, and in the middle of his scream he managed to pull the trigger of his pistol upon the Seventh Bullet that had to save him from four days of worse than hell.

And the Seventh Bullet, which belonged to the devil, missed fire.

2468874

Made in the USA